SWEET TIME

A SUGAR RUSH ROMANCE

NINA LANE

SNOW QUEEN
PUBLISHING

Sweet Time
A Sugar Rush Romance

Published by Snow Queen Publishing

This book is a work of fiction. All names, characters, locations, and incidents are products of the author's imagination, or have been used fictitiously. Any resemblance to actual persons living or dead, locales, or events is entirely coincidental.

Cover photography: Kelsey Keeton
Cover design: Perfect Pear Creative Covers

ISBN: 978-1-954185-00-5

SWEET TIME
Nina Lane

&

Vibrant, flirty Mia is pink glitter and rainbows. Security chief
Gavin is steel and pain. What happens when their worlds collide?

Warning!
Contains caramel coffee with rainbow sprinkles, fairy coloring
books, Rodents Of Unusual Size, and a hot, controlling hero who
does dirty things with a whoopie pie.

The Sugar Rush books are sexy contemporary romances by New
York Times bestselling author Nina Lane. They can be read as
standalones or enjoyed as a series.

SWEET DREAMS
SWEET ESCAPE
SWEET SURRENDER
SWEET TIME
SWEET LIFE

www.ninalane.com

CHAPTER 1

*H*e was a hell of a nut to crack.

A tall, broad-shouldered, square-jawed, sexy-in-a-stoic-way, strong silent type, impossibly *hard* nut to crack.

And Mia Donovan considered herself to be a world-class nutcracker—in the best possible way, of course. She wanted to open that man up and discover all the mysteries hiding behind his inflexible, rigid exterior.

But Gavin Knight, impassive owner of Knight Security, wouldn't let her close enough to even touch him, let alone crack him open. He didn't find her worthy of the slightest bit of attention, even though he'd never bothered getting to know her.

Even though he didn't notice anything about her. Not her tight sweaters, short skirts, and floral tights. Not her long blond hair, which had drawn compliments since she was in kindergarten. Not even her patently obvious attempts to flirt with him.

She gave him a mild glower, just to see if he'd at least feel her stare. Nothing.

As usual, he sat at a window table in the Wild Child Bakery, a boring cup of black coffee near his elbow and not a single éclair or chocolate truffle anywhere in his vicinity. His attention was focused on his sleek laptop, his expression solemn behind the wire-rimmed glasses that couldn't hide the striking blue of his eyes.

Also as usual, his profile was sheer perfection—his sharp cheekbones sloped down to a cut-glass jaw and beautifully shaped mouth. Even his dark hair was in on the effect—brushed away from his forehead with the short cut emphasizing the strong lines of his face.

Also as usual, he wore black trousers and a black shirt with the Knight Security logo over the breast pocket. *Also* as usual, the shirt fit him to such delicious perfection, stretching over his muscular chest and around his bulging biceps, that Mia's mouth watered.

Darn it. She'd been trying to wean herself off her year-long attraction to him. If he didn't want to notice her, then screw him. She had enough attention from other boys.

The problem was she didn't want a *boy*. She wanted a man. More specifically, a man named Gavin Knight who, despite his statue-like demeanor, was intensely hard-working and sexy as all hell. He'd gotten her hot and tingly the second he'd walked into Wild Child with his steel briefcase to install a security system.

Even now, a year later, her belly fluttered at the sight of him. Apparently her body didn't know when to quit, even if her mind was determined to stop drooling over him once and for all.

"Here you go." Polly Lockhart, Mia's best friend and owner of Wild Child, stopped by the table. She set a frothy caramel-choco-late mochaccino, topped with a pile of sprinkles-laced whipped cream, in front of Mia. "Want another muffin?"

"No, thanks." Mia gestured to the portfolio of bridal hairstyles she'd been perusing. "Do you want to take this to Julia and show her which ones you like?"

"And risk her wrath? No way. She has her own ideas about my wedding day hair and makeup, and I have no intention of getting in her way."

"I know, but it's your hair and makeup. What if she does something you don't like?"

Polly waved her hand dismissively. "No one is a better stylist than my future aunt-in-law, as she'll tell you herself. I consider it a win that she hasn't taken over the entire wedding, so I'm happy to let her have her way with my hair and makeup. Have you picked up your dress yet?"

"Friday." Mia arranged the portfolios into a little stack. "The dressmaker called for a final fitting. Then I'm meeting the caterer at the villa to go over the new layout of the reception."

"Are you sure you're okay with all this?" Polly's forehead creased. "It's my fault for biting off more than I could chew, but it's not too late to hire someone to take over. I want you to enjoy yourself too, not have to work all the time."

"Polly." Mia squeezed her friend's hand. "I'm happy to do this for you. Besides, I have all the plans and know exactly what you want. Remember when we were ten and I planned a wedding for Mr. Elephant and Miss Monkey? This is a bigger version of that."

Polly smiled. "And without a mud cake and rainwater champagne, right? I know you can do it, but I also know this wedding has grown to rather epic proportions. So if it's getting overwhelming, please tell me."

"Everything is under control, I promise."

Polly gave her a hug filled with gratitude, then headed back to the counter. Mia turned her attention to the bridal hairstyles portfolio.

She hadn't started out as command central for her friend's upcoming nuptials to Luke Stone, CEO of the Sugar Rush Candy Company. But she would allow nothing to ruin the most important day in Polly's life, not to mention a Stone brother's wedding.

The eldest of five brothers and a sister, Luke Stone was the second-in-line, after patriarch Warren Stone, of Indigo Bay's wealthiest, most prominent family. Founded by a Stone ancestor in the mid-nineteenth century, the historic Sugar Rush Candy

Company had changed the economic landscape of the coastal California town and continued to be the dominant force both commercially and socially. The public was waiting with bated breath for the extravagant wedding of the first Stone brother.

Given the Stone family wealth, Luke could have hired Martha Stewart and her crew to plan the whole affair. But he wanted whatever Polly wanted, and Polly had been adamant about planning the wedding herself, with sister Hannah and Mia's help.

None of them had been surprised—thanks to her mother's influence, Polly had always been an advocate for personal involvement, and she'd turned Wild Child around from near bankruptcy into a major success.

But a few months ago, Polly had started to struggle with running one branch of Wild Child, opening another in Indigo Bay, and planning an early fall wedding all at the same time. So Mia had taken control of the wedding details to give her friend some room to breathe. Polly trusted her wholeheartedly with the task, and Mia had no intention of letting her down.

The good news was that just invoking the Stone name produced results, not to mention there was a virtually unlimited budget. The family also owned the venue—a sprawling Spanish villa on a cliff overlooking the ocean—so Mia had been serving as the coordinator of the vendors, confirming details about the flowers and décor, and reorganizing the reception to accommodate all the guests. As Polly's maid of honor, she wouldn't be coordinating everything on the day of the event, but the villa manager would ensure it all ran smoothly.

Though the stakes were high—Luke's family ran with a high-class crowd who would be anticipating the best—Mia was enjoying the challenge. Aside from being thrilled for Luke and Polly, the wedding had taken her mind off the stark fact that she'd have to start job hunting soon or risk atrophying in her tiny cubicle at the insurance agency.

She took a sip of her mochaccino and sighed. She could practically hear her granny bemoaning the fact that Mia was stuck in the exact kind of dead-end job she'd always tried so hard to avoid. Even her attempts to liven up the insurance reports had fallen flat. She'd already gotten in trouble twice for drawing little flowers on the invoices and using bubbles instead of dots over the *I*'s.

Mia's phone buzzed. She shook off her brief malaise and pulled up a text from her friend Susan: *Drinks @ Rave on Dandelion St. 5pm – be there!*

"Hey, Polly, can you make it to happy hour?" Mia gestured to her phone. "Susan just texted. New bar on Dandelion."

"I can't, I'm sorry. Luke's brother Adam is coming home, and we're going out with him, Hannah, and Evan."

Though Mia had half-expected a negative response, she couldn't suppress a stab of disappointment. Happy hour aside, she and Polly hadn't done anything together in weeks. Polly spent all her evenings with Luke now, and when they went out, it was often with Hannah and Evan. Cute little foursome, two brothers and two sisters.

Mia had tried not to feel left out, but it wasn't always easy. Especially since Polly had met Luke when Mia dragged her out for drinks on her birthday. She couldn't help feeling a bit like she'd been the matchmaker.

Still, she was genuinely happy for Polly, and she figured things would get back to normal after the excitement of the wedding.

"Miss Donovan."

The deep, rumbling voice skittered rather deliciously down her spine. Mia looked straight up into the unreadable face of Gavin Knight, who was standing right beside her table.

Her mind went blank. He'd actually approached her? He knew her last name? What alternate universe had she just fallen into?

"We need to talk," he said.

Mia could only stare at him, like he was a brick wall come to life. Though given his lack of response to her flirtations—which had never failed on any other man—he sort of was.

She dug deep to find a nonchalant, *whatever* tone of voice. "What is it we need to talk about, Mr. Knight?"

He pulled a chair away from the table and sat down. His knee bumped against hers. Her heartbeat skyrocketed.

Was this really happening? All those months of ignoring her and now he was taking a seat? Should she be excited or annoyed? She chose the latter.

"We need to discuss the layout and plans for Luke and Polly's wedding." Gavin set his laptop on the table. "I'm personally handling the security for the event. My understanding is that you've taken charge of all the plans."

"That's correct."

"A situation has come to light that requires further evaluation of our security operations."

Mia frowned. "What kind of *situation*?"

"I'm not at liberty to discuss the details with you, but it means I need to reevaluate both internal and external areas of the venue." He opened his laptop. "I've briefed Luke on the situation and have his full authorization to do whatever is necessary to ensure the safety of everyone at the wedding."

Alarm rustled in her. "Is there some sort of danger?"

"As I said, I'm not at liberty to provide details. The point is that I understand the guest list has grown, and there are a number of vendors involved in the reception. I need to see all the updated plans. I need the latest guest list, the seating chart, the vendors, photographer, and music contact list, and the timeline. I also want to know exactly what kind of decorations are planned."

Mia folded her arms, her alarm quickly replaced by irritation. "Decorations? Are you leaving the personal security business and going into wedding planning?"

He was unperturbed by her sharp tone. "I will be increasing

the security level at the venue, which means revaluating the full set-up. I don't want to concern Polly with this matter."

"Damned right you won't *concern Polly*," Mia replied tersely. "She is my best friend, and this is her dream wedding. You will not upset her with talk about security levels and revaluations."

"I don't intend to." Gavin studied the laptop screen. "As I understand it, you have all the details. Therefore, I need the information from you so I can make necessary changes."

"What kind of changes?"

"I'll know when I see the updated plans. When can I have them?"

Mia eyed him suspiciously. The Stones were so high profile that personal security was the norm for them. But it was not the norm for free-spirited Polly, who'd spent her childhood on a commune before her mother had opened Wild Child, a bohemian bakery that had become a gathering point for artists and musicians.

After her mother's death, Polly had revived the bakery with Luke's help, and now Wild Child boasted successful branches in both the farming community of Rainsville and the upscale coastal town of Indigo Bay.

Polly, being both trusting and dedicated to retaining her mother's vision of a warm, welcoming collective, had even balked at the idea of installing state-of-the-art security systems in the bakery, though Gavin and Luke had eventually overruled her.

But if she thought her family and friends were somehow at risk at her wedding, of all places, she would likely call the whole thing off and convince Luke to elope. Not only would that be a social disaster, it wouldn't go over well at all with the rest of the Stones. Certainly it would be no way for Polly to start her new married life.

Mia leaned forward to look Gavin in the eye.

"Look, Mr. Knight," she said coldly. "I've known Polly since we were ten years old. She is the kindest, most caring, and unaffected woman you'll ever meet. She would do anything for anyone. And I'm the only person in the world who knows that since childhood, she has secretly dreamed of a fairy tale wedding to the love of her life. There is no way in hell I will let you do anything to ruin that for her."

He studied her for a moment. Was that admiration flickering in his blue eyes? Surely not from the man who was about as expressive as a clam.

But of course she was mistaken. Nothing showed in Gavin's eyes except a deep, cobalt blue almost startling in intensity, a blue that reminded her of sea-glass, arctic glaciers, slivers of agate—

See? He's hard and icy all the way through. You can stop imagining things that aren't there.

"I don't intend to ruin anything for anyone." Gavin turned his attention back to his laptop. "My sole purpose is to keep everyone safe. My team is also well instructed on the importance of remaining unobtrusive, which is precisely the reason I intend to carry out necessary changes in advance of the event."

God, the man spoke like a machine. Mia picked up her mug, suddenly glad he'd ignored her all these months. She shouldn't have wasted her time on him.

She sipped her coffee drink, appreciating the chocolate-caramel sweetness. A crease appeared between Gavin's eyebrows as he studied the tall mug loaded with whipped cream and rainbow sprinkles.

"What exactly is that?" he asked.

"Caramel-chocolate mochaccino with extra chocolate, a shot of toffee syrup, vanilla whipped cream, and rainbow sprinkles." Mia lifted her chin in defiance, daring him to make fun of her. "It's not on the menu. I invented it myself, and Polly's nice enough to make me one whenever I come in."

He said nothing, only regarded her in silence.

"What?" she asked irritably.

"Whipped cream." He gestured to her mouth.

Mia grabbed a napkin, then decided to screw with the brick-wall man just one more time. Out of habit, of course. She met his gaze and flicked her tongue out slowly to lick the cream off her lips.

"Better?" she asked.

He nodded and turned back to his laptop. Frustration tightened her chest, even though she was supposed to be *done with him*.

"You can finish this." She pushed the mochaccino toward him and stood. "Maybe it'll sweeten you up."

"I only drink black coffee."

"Of course you do." She rolled her eyes, but of course he wasn't looking at her. "With not even one sugar. Look, I need to go. I have plans tonight."

So there. She couldn't help hoping he'd ask what *kind* of plans she had, but he didn't. As usual.

"I need the details and list of changes from you." He removed a business card from his briefcase and put it on the table. "You can email them to me at this address."

Sure. For months, he couldn't even spare her a glance, but now that he wanted something from her, he was giving her his contact info.

She picked up the portfolio and slung her bag over her shoulder. She walked away from him without looking back.

About time Mr. Gavin Knight had a taste of his own damned medicine.

CHAPTER 2

*N*oise masquerading as music thumped against Mia's ears. She squeezed closer to Susan to make room for Anne at the table that was about the size of a quarter and covered with a mysterious sticky substance.

"This place is smaller than I thought," Susan yelled above the screech of the band.

"And more crowded," Mia agreed, though she suspected the jam-packed crowd was due to the two-dollar beers rather than the atmosphere.

"Hi, ladies." A young man with curly brown hair approached. His tie was askew against his wrinkled shirt. "Fancy seeing you all here."

"Danny!" Anne pushed closer to Mia to make a space for him to sit. "Come on and join us."

He sat, thumping his pint of ale on the table and nearly knocking over Susan's margarita. Mia caught the glass and pushed it back on the table.

"Sorry." Danny grinned at her, his eyes sparkling. "You look especially lovely tonight, Mia."

Susan elbowed her in the side and wiggled her eyebrows none

too discreetly. Mia returned Danny's smile. They'd frequented the same bars over the past few months, but hadn't yet socialized beyond that. He was the kind of boy she'd always liked—cute and engaging with a ready smile. A recent grad of San Francisco State, he was also in a similar *"what next?"* stage of life as she was, so they had a lot to commiserate about.

"Any luck with the job search?" she asked.

"Applied at a new upstart in San Jose." He tilted his head back for a swallow of beer. "You?"

Mia shook her head. "Planning Luke and Polly's wedding has taken up so much time that I haven't been able to job hunt much. I'll have to start soon, though."

She wasn't looking forward to it, either. She was bound to feel a little dispirited after the wedding was over and Polly no longer needed her help. She'd offered to help cover shifts at Wild Child when Polly and Luke were on their honeymoon, but that would only last so long.

"Hey, I have some leads you might be interested in," Danny remarked. "Or you could totally get into modeling or acting."

She lifted her eyebrows in a *"really?"* look, which he responded to with an abashed smile.

"Sorry." He took a swig of the ale. "I lay it on thick when I get nervous around a beautiful girl. But you could totally be a model," he added hastily. "I mean that sincerely."

"Thank you." Mia shifted to try and escape Susan's persistent elbow nudges. "Sincerely."

She glanced at her watch. Any other night, she might have suggested they all head to a different bar—one without sticky tables and watered-down drinks—but she had to work the following day and there was still so much to do for the wedding.

"I'm going to head out." She picked up her purse and squeezed out of the chair. "I have stuff I should finish up at home. Everyone, have a good evening."

A chorus of goodbyes followed her as she headed out to her

car. Usually being out with her friends eased her growing uncertainty about her life, but tonight she felt worse.

Five years from now, would she still be working at the insurance agency, watching the clock until she could leave at five and head directly to happy hour in a dank, crowded bar?

She didn't want a life like that. It was painfully close to the one her parents had lived, except they'd never even enjoyed happy hour. They'd had dead-end jobs, tedious routines, and a stale marriage held together by sheer inertia.

Granny hadn't wanted Mia to live that kind of life either, encouraging her to "follow her heart" and "create beauty" when her parents had dictated that she become a business or economics major.

She'd seized her grandmother's advice with both hands, determined to burst through life in a shower of glitter and sparkles. Too late, she'd discovered that glitter and sparkles didn't pay the bills. And she had yet to find any jobs seeking applicants who were "good at following your heart" or "an excellent beauty creator."

After returning to her apartment, Mia showered, painted her toenails a shiny purple, and watched the Miracle Max scene from *The Princess Bride* because "to blave" always made her smile. She was just getting herself a bowl of ice cream when a knock came at the door.

She set the bowl on the kitchen counter and went to peer through the peephole. Her heart jumped.

Gavin Knight stood on the doorstep. She tightened the belt of her bathrobe and yanked open the door.

She ignored the way her pulse sped up at the sight of him—all big and masculine with his steel briefcase and square-jawed, stoic expression. His wire-rimmed glasses softened the hard lines of his face only slightly, giving him a Clark Kentish vibe that appealed to all the parts of her that loved secrets and alter egos. Not to mention nerdy superheroes.

Reminding herself of all the times he'd ignored her, she hardened her still-simmering attraction to him. "Yes?"

Gavin's blue gaze skittered over her floral cotton robe, as if he hadn't expected to see her undressed. It was eleven p.m., for god's sake. What had he expected?

"Yes?" she repeated.

"I apologize for bothering you," he said. "I left the office later than I expected. I need the wedding plans. You didn't email them to me."

"I don't have them online," Mia replied. "Polly and I have all the plans in binders and folders. Which you are absolutely not taking from me."

"Then I'll review them now and make copies tomorrow."

His voice was implacable, like he had no intention of moving from her doorstep until he'd gotten what he came for.

"I'm sorry," she said sharply. "But I'm busy at the moment."

"I'll wait."

Good god, he was serious. He planted his feet apart, his shoulders squaring. He didn't move closer to her, remaining a good distance away as if he didn't want to threaten or scare her with his imposing presence.

Not that he would have. She'd been irritated with him for ignoring her flirtations, and now she was getting downright mad over his persistence about the wedding, but he radiated a strong, protective authority that she'd liked *so much* from the moment he'd first walked into Wild Child. She could never be scared of him.

She could, however, be peevish with him.

"Come in, then." With a huff, she stepped aside, pulling the door open wider. "The sooner we get this over with, the better."

He entered and cast a quick, assessing glance around at her French Country décor with the vases of dried flowers, vintage floral chairs, distressed bookshelves, and the comfy, sky-blue sofa laden with heart-shaped pillows and stuffed animals.

Not that he was looking at the actual furnishings, of course. Probably he was looking for possible security issues like a broken window lock or a lurking Kryptonite-powered supervillain.

"Well, sit down," Mia ordered inhospitably, gesturing to the white farmhouse table in the kitchen.

He sat, his big frame and black shirt incongruous in the feminine surroundings. He removed his laptop from the briefcase and set it on the table. Mia collected an armful of binders from the bookshelf. Each one represented months of hard work and research they'd done to ensure Polly had the wedding of her dreams.

She started toward the table when Gavin pushed his chair back and stood. She paused, somewhat taken aback by how much room he took up in her little kitchen.

He retrieved her abandoned bowl of ice cream from the counter, set it at the place across from him, and sat back down.

What...?

"You'd better eat that before it melts," he remarked mildly.

Mia shook off a silly sense of pleasure over the gesture. It had to be professional instinct that compelled him to notice little things like that. Being perceptive and observant were probably the top qualities required in a security operative.

She was just surprised that he'd noticed her ice cream considering he'd barely ever noticed *her*.

She plunked the binders down one by one on the table.

"This one is for budgeting and receipts. This one is for gown and bridesmaid dress samples, and pictures of different hairstyles. This one is wedding guests, invitations, and seating charts. This one is for caterers, musicians, and photographers. This one is the timeline for the ceremony, and the schedule of events. This one was supposed to be for the honeymoon, but Luke wanted it to be a surprise for Polly so he's doing all the planning. So I'm using this binder for Polly's packing list and the Wild Child schedule, so she doesn't have to worry about the bakery while she's away."

Gavin eyed the multiple binders. Mia couldn't tell if he was impressed with her organizational skills or if he thought she'd gone way over the top.

Not that she cared what he thought, anyway.

She sat down and picked up the bowl of ice cream. The hostess in her wanted to offer him something to eat or drink, but given the way he'd barged in here at this hour and without advance warning...he didn't deserve her hospitality. Or her ice cream. Or her.

She ate a spoonful of ice cream and watched him open the first binder. His strong features were set with serious concentration, though up close the wire-rimmed glasses softened the hard lines of his face a bit more. He wrote something on a legal pad, his penmanship compact and precise. She liked the way he held his pen, close to the point with a firm grip.

Her belly fluttered, even as she groaned inwardly. Despite trying to steel herself against him, everything about Gavin Knight still made her go all warm and melty inside. She'd thought her attraction to him was based on the fact that he was one of the few men who hadn't fallen for her charms—but over the months she'd realized it was more than that. She liked his strength, his dedication, the loyalty he commanded from his team of security operatives.

Of course, she didn't like his immunity to her, which was the reason she had to stop flirting with him. A girl had to know when to quit, after all.

"I'm reevaluating the existing plans." He unfolded a piece of paper and spread it out on the table between them. "This is a diagram of the villa and surrounding grounds."

Mia leaned forward to look at the map of the sprawling villa where the wedding would be held before the guests moved to the reception hall. Red and blue lines indicated the guest route and parking areas.

"What are the circles around the grounds?" she asked.

"I've implemented three rings of security around the perimeter of the venue." Gavin pointed to the largest circle. "Outer, middle, and interior. The interior is the tightest."

"I would hope so." Her voice came out husky.

Oh, Mia. So much for not flirting.

CHAPTER 3

*S*he was off limits. He'd been telling himself that for the
past year.

Every. Fucking. Time.

Every time he saw her in her short little skirts and tight
sweaters, her thick blond hair falling like spun silk down her
back. Every time she made a suggestive comment in her honeyed
voice, her body almost vibrating with a plea for his response.
Every time his guard slipped and he caught himself staring at her
round ass or her perfectly shaped lips.

Every time he imagined those lips wrapped around his cock.

Off limits, Knight.

She hadn't been off limits in his head. There, he'd done a
thousand dirty things to her—twisted her hair around his fist,
pulled her head back, and devoured her rosebud mouth. Turned
her around and spread her over the arm of the sofa to fuck her
from behind. Ordered her to spread her legs and finger herself
for him. Watched her twist her nipples as he came on her tits.

More than once he'd been tempted to break all his rules and
teach her a lesson. Put her over his knee, lift up her skirt, and
spank her for being a tease.

She'd been an increasingly painful test of his self-control. Only his dedication to Luke Stone and his family, which would soon officially include Polly Lockhart, prevented Gavin from crossing the line. As Polly's best friend, Mia was close enough to the family that he'd kept his distance.

Tough to keep his distance when she was this close, though. Close enough that he could smell her sweet, citrusy scent. See the flicker of her tongue as she closed her mouth around a spoonful of ice cream. Her proximity was distracting.

At the bakery he could always sit a few tables away from her. He disliked acknowledging he needed a physical barrier from a seemingly harmless, fairy-like girl, but the more he saw her breasts rounding out her sweaters or her long legs in flower-patterned tights...the less he trusted his restraint.

Even now, his blood was on low simmer. He was trained to read people, to anticipate danger, to let nothing get in the way of keeping his principals safe. Not even his longstanding friendship with Luke had affected his ability to do his job. In some ways, his personal bond to the Stone family had intensified his effectiveness.

Not that he was searching for a justification to start up with the blonde beauty sitting across from him.

"Any public spectators will be restricted from entering the outer ring." He tapped his pen on the map again. "I'll be working with local law enforcement to provide a visible presence outside the venue. Has anything changed in the reception floor plan?"

"We added a few more tables to accommodate all the guests."

"I'll need to see the seating arrangements. And the entry procedure from parking to the venue is far too long and complicated. I will also be strengthening the parking control measures."

"Well, the reason for the entry procedure is that guests need to walk from the parking lot to the courtyard," Mia informed him, a sarcastic bite to her tone. "And Julia Bennett wanted them to enter through a wing of the villa that isn't usually opened to the public. Like entering the Sistine Chapel through the Vatican museums."

For Christ's sake. Gavin barely suppressed a snort.

"That's the way she described it, anyway," Mia said.

He glanced at her, gauging that she wasn't too intimidated by the beautiful and formidable Julia Bennett. The sister of Warren Stone's late wife, Julia was a force to be reckoned with.

Unexpectedly, Gavin liked the idea that Mia Donovan could hold her own against the older woman.

"Sistine Chapel or not," he said. "For security purposes, the route needs to be simplified."

He took a red pen out of his briefcase and drew a line from the parking lot, up the slope toward the villa.

"The wedding is in two weeks," Mia said. "Polly assured me you and Luke went over all the details."

"We did. The situation has changed."

"How?"

He sensed her curiosity bubbling just beneath the surface. Not surprising. He'd seen her interacting with people at Wild Child plenty of times. She was lively and eager, wanting to know everything about everyone.

"I'll worry about that part," he said. "You just need to do what I say."

She frowned, crossing her arms over her chest. Her robe gaped open at the neck, revealing a V of pale skin leading down to her round breasts. He'd noticed them enough times to gauge they were big enough to fit in his hands perfectly. He was tempted to slip his pen into the neckline of her robe and pull it down to expose her cleavage. His groin tightened.

"Is Polly in danger?" she asked.

"I don't want any guests delayed at the entry point." He tapped his pen on the map. "I'm allocating two more security officers for access control and five more to patrol the exterior during the ceremony."

"Great. The guests will love seeing security dudes at a family wedding."

"They will be dressed appropriately," Gavin said. "My men know how to blend in at any event. And we will do a thorough sweep of the grounds before anyone arrives."

"Really." Mia's voice held a sudden note of strain.

He looked at her. Concern darkened her green eyes, and her jaw was tense.

"Is Polly in danger?" she repeated.

Tough question. He considered before answering. He didn't want to lie to her, but he also didn't want to scare her. And he needed to confine the details to the small circle of people involved in the case.

"When you marry into a family as prominent as the Stones, you expose yourself to a certain level of risk," he finally said. "But that's the point of my job. To mitigate the risks. To ensure they never reach the level of actual danger."

Her forehead was still creased with worry. A sudden, hard need to protect her rose in him. Before he could stop himself, he reached across the table to put his hand over hers.

"No one will get hurt," he said. "Not on my watch."

She looked at his hand engulfing hers. If she was reassured, she didn't say so. Instead, she withdrew her hand from under his and scooped up another spoonful of ice cream.

"And not as long as I do what you say, right?" she asked.

His blood simmered at the thought of her *doing what he said*. Like turning around and lifting up her skirt to show him her pert little ass. Or getting on her knees to suck his cock.

"Correct." He turned his attention back to the map. His palm was still warm from the heat of her hand.

She shifted, flicking her long hair over her shoulder. He felt the rustle of her body as if she'd moved against him. Was she wearing underwear?

"I need an updated program and timeline." He focused on

his laptop. "And guest list. I've done background checks on all the vendors, but if there have been any changes, I need to know about them now. *No one*, not even a delivery guy, gets past the gates unless I've personally cleared them. Understand?"

"Yes, sir."

That *"sir"* spoken in her honeyed voice made his dick twitch. He shifted his gaze to her. She was watching him with faint amusement.

"You're really like this, huh?" she asked.

"Like what?"

"This." She waved her hand around the air in front of him. "All serious and rigid."

"My job is serious and rigid."

"Your *job*." She rested her chin on her hand and studied him. "What about you?"

He stifled a humorless laugh. A girl like her didn't need to know anything about him. Didn't need his polluted life staining her pretty little world.

"What about me?" he finally asked.

"Do you know I've never seen you smile? All these months that you've been coming into Wild Child, not once have I seen you smile."

That was almost surprising. With her silly flirting and constant talk about "having fun," she'd made him smile countless times—to himself, at least.

He looked at her—peaches and cream, golden hair, blinking at him with those big doe eyes. A surprisingly real, easy smile formed on his lips.

She stared back at him, surprise flashing in her expression before a responding smile bloomed across her face. Suddenly his world filled with sunlight.

Gavin dropped his smile before he was tempted to just sit there grinning at her like a buffoon.

"Now you can cross that off your bucket list." He turned his attention back to the binders.

"You have a really nice smile, Gavin," Mia remarked. "You should lead with that."

"Instead of?"

"Instead of this stern Roman emperor thing you've got going on." She rose, picking up her empty bowl of ice cream. "Do you want anything to drink? I can make you my famous caramel-chocolate mochaccino so you can have a delicious taste of something besides *black coffee, no sugar*."

"No, thank you."

"What about ice cream? I have chocolate chip or strawberry, but I'm guessing you don't eat ice cream, do you?"

"I do not."

She rolled her eyes and snarkily mouthed the words *"I do not"* as she opened the freezer and took out a carton of chocolate chip. Little brat. Again he had the urge to turn her over his knee and spank her for being sassy. A fantasy he'd jacked off to more than once.

From the corner of his eye, he watched her scoop more ice cream into her bowl. Her robe was pale blue with little flowers, the hem falling to her knees and leaving her smooth calves bare. The knot in the belt was starting to come loose. One tug and he could pull it right off her, see if she wore anything underneath.

Shit. He was getting hard.

Mia closed the freezer and returned to the table with her bowl. She caught his glance and smiled ruefully.

"Late dinner," she said. "A friend and I went to check out this new bar for happy hour after work, but it turned out to be a dive with dirty tables and warm beer. Needless to say, we cut the evening short."

Gavin's shoulders tensed. He disliked the vague term *a friend*.

"What kind of friend?" he asked.

"Why, Mr. Knight." Mia ate a spoonful of ice cream, her

eyebrows lifting. "Are you asking because you're a teensy bit jealous that the *friend* might have been of the male species?"

Irritation scraped his insides. "I am not."

"The friend was Susan." Mia sighed, mushing the ice cream with her spoon. "I haven't had a boyfriend in, like, a year. Just a bunch of college boy dating. Which is totally fun, but predictable, you know?"

"I do not."

The thought of her dating "a bunch" of horny college boys, however...that made him want to break something.

"Given your penchant for flirting, I'm surprised the *boys* aren't lined up at your door," he said.

"Oh, I get a lot of offers." She waved her spoon in the air and spoke without conceit, as if she were merely stating a fact. "But none of them are really interesting. I guess it's okay because I like to go out and have fun, but...I don't know. A year ago, Polly was at this total dead end, and now look at her with Luke and her business and everything. Our friend Jessica just got engaged, and our other friend Mary moved to New York last month to take a job with a news agency. It kind of sucks when your friends are doing all this cool stuff, and your big news is that you went to a new blues club with Johnny, who's in his fifth year at San Jose State and wants to be a musician because he's been playing saxophone for a full week."

She fell silent, staring at her bowl before looking up at him with a grimace.

"Way to spill my guts, huh?" A pink flush rose to her cheeks. "Sorry. I have no idea where that all came from. So what...you need the reception floor plan or something?"

He stood, pushing his chair back. Mia blinked up at him, her eyes green as a forest. He opened the refrigerator. A pizza box, a few cans of soda, and a jar of peanut butter sat on the shelves.

"Is this usually how your fridge is stocked?" he asked.

"I eat out a lot."

"And when you're home, you eat ice cream and other junk."

Her eyebrows snapped together. "What do you care?"

What *did* he care? He wasn't into analyzing his psyche, but over the past year, he'd grown unwillingly fond of Mia Donovan. He hadn't wanted to admit it, but he'd looked forward to seeing her whenever he went into Wild Child. If she wasn't there, he'd been disappointed.

In her short skirts and sweaters, twirling a lock of blond hair around her finger, swinging her crossed leg, leaning too close to him at the counter, batting her long eyelashes at him...fuck if he hadn't started to enjoy that. To enjoy *her*.

"It's important that you eat right," he said.

She rolled her eyes. "Thanks for the advice, Daddy."

He closed the refrigerator. The "daddy" affected him even more than the "sir" had, spearing him with both heat and steely possessiveness.

"It's not advice," he said. "It's a statement of fact."

"Let me guess." She tossed her hair over her shoulder with a scoff. "You live by *statements of fact* and a rigid routine. You eat the same thing every day, meals carefully calibrated to maximize their nutritional impact, you have a daily workout regimen that you do first thing in the morning, you arrive at work at the exact same time every day, and you follow a strict schedule utterly devoid of surprises."

She'd hit the mark too close for his comfort. Much as he needed his routine and schedule, he disliked the reminder that she enjoyed ice cream for dinner and spontaneity.

"Surprises are a menace," he said. "Routine is not."

"A *menace*?" She laughed, the sound like little silver bells. "What about surprise parties or presents?"

He shook his head. "Not for me."

"Really? Why not?"

"You can't prepare for a surprise," Gavin said. "You can't plan or offer input. They come out of nowhere, and you're forced to react in a way you might not want to. You have no control over a surprise."

"That's the *point*."

"That's why I don't like them."

She huffed out an exasperated laugh and turned back to her ice cream, crossing her legs in a way that made her robe slide up on her thigh. His gaze went to the golden length of her leg, his hand twitching with the urge to stroke her smooth skin.

Hell if he didn't want to discover all *her* surprises.

He forced his gaze back to her face. She watched him with a playful expression, like she knew exactly the effect she had on him. Of course she did, the little minx. She swirled her tongue around the spoon, licking up the ice cream dripping down the handle. Lust snapped through him, the strike of a whip.

"So what makes Control Freak Gavin Knight *lose* control, hmm?" Mia asked.

"Keep licking the spoon like that and you'll find out." His voice was rough, edged with self-restraint.

"You mean like this?" Mia batted her eyelashes at him as she licked her way back to the top of the spoon.

Gavin shook his head, torn between wanting to give her more ice cream or hauling her into his arms and kissing her senseless.

"Brat," he murmured.

"Spoilsport who doesn't know surprises are what makes life *fun*."

She dropped the spoon back into the bowl and rose to set it in the sink.

Her sweet, vanilla scent filled his head. Her robe gaped open more, exposing the curve of her breast. His blood heated into full boil.

She turned, her gaze colliding with his. A smear of ice cream decorated her upper lip. He wanted to finally taste that rosebud mouth.

He unclenched his hand from the refrigerator door handle

and reached for the front of her robe. Her eyes widened. He fisted the material and pulled her closer until a few scant inches separated them.

"You like to tease me, don't you?" His body tensed at her nearness, his dick pressing against the fly of his trousers.

Her throat rippled with a swallow. Uncertainty flashed in her expression, as if she were suddenly questioning whether it had been a good idea to push him this far.

"Well, you're just so...*hard*," she said. "No man has ever ignored me the way you do. I was just waiting for something to happen."

He lifted his other hand to cup her chin. "And what did you hope would happen, honey?"

"I guess I just wanted your attention." She scowled, wrinkling her cute little nose. "Past tense. *Wanted*. Maybe I don't like you anymore."

"I doubt that."

She rolled her eyes. "Oh, so *now* you think you know what I like and don't like?"

"You like vanilla cupcakes and the color pink. You like boys with curly hair, margaritas, Zumba, and a band called the Riders. Your favorite book is *The Secret Garden*, your favorite restaurant is Lotus Indian Cuisine, and your favorite movie is *The Princess Bride*. You like music apps, Dungeness crab, penguins, a show called *Curlicue*, and the Japanese tea garden in Golden Gate Park. You also like helping your friends and being loyal."

Mia stared at him. "How do you know all that?"

"A year of noticing you."

"I thought you barely knew I existed."

He bit back a laugh. "I know you exist. In fact, you have my full, undivided attention. So now what?"

And what the hell was he getting himself into?

ow what?

She had no idea. Her mind was blank.

All she could do was stand there with his hand fisted in her robe and his blue eyes pinning her to the spot. She'd had countless fantasies about what might happen the day Gavin Knight finally noticed her—fantasies ranging from him fucking her powerfully on the bakery counter to them walking off arm in arm to share a chocolate milkshake.

She'd never once imagined them standing in her tiny kitchen, the air thick, with Gavin holding her in place and asking what happened next.

The heavy silence stretched into an eternity. She was trapped in his gaze, like a butterfly caught in a jar. His expression was as unreadable as ever, but the cadence of his breathing had shifted and a pulse ticked visibly in his jaw.

She'd gotten to him. After all this time, maybe she was about to discover that security operative Gavin Knight wasn't quite as impassive as he'd always seemed.

"Now…" She darted her tongue out to lick her lips. "Now you can kiss me."

Her heart beat wildly. His eyes darkened. For an instant, she thought he'd shake his head and move away, call her a silly girl, but instead he drew her closer with a firm grip.

Her breathing grew shallow. She lifted her hands tentatively to his chest. Pleasure washed through her. His hard, solid muscles beneath her fingers and the body heat that flowed clear up her arms sent her reeling. He felt better than she'd imagined, and she yearned to slide her hands under his shirt, touch the taut, bare skin of his abs...

Like an eagle swooping to a nest, he lowered his head and slanted his mouth across hers. There was no fumbling, no hesitation, no uncertainty. Gavin Knight was a man who knew how to take what he wanted.

And take her he did—urging her lips apart, sliding his tongue into her mouth, tasting every part of her. He moved his hands to the sides of her neck and up to cradle her head, tilting her face to just the right angle so he could plunder her mouth with his.

Mia's knees went weak. She tightened her fingers on his shirtfront, her whole body swaying toward him. Everything inside her came alive—blood pulsing, nerves firing, heart pounding. In all the times she'd imagined him kissing her, she'd never dreamed it could be so exhilarating and frightening at the same time. Like she was falling, spinning downward into a galaxy of stars without knowing where she would land.

He moved one hand from her neck and unfastened the belt of her robe.

Oh my god...a moan escaped her as his strong, callused hands caressed the bare skin of her midriff. Aside from a pair of pink bikini panties, she was naked. A hint of anxiety coiled inside her.

He lifted his head from hers. He grabbed her wrists and placed her hands behind her on the counter. Her robe fell open fully, revealing her bare breasts, the curve of her waist, her taut belly hugged by the pink cotton of her panties. Gavin stepped away and raked his gaze over her body as if he were about to devour her.

Probably he was. Her breathing quickened. She'd never been shy about her body, but with *him* staring at her like that, radiating experience and potent masculine heat, a wave of self-consciousness struck her.

"Pretty." He drew one finger between her breasts all the way down to the edge of her panties. "Do you wax?"

She squirmed. A flush rose to her cheeks. "Yes."

An approving rumble sounded deep in his chest, like a lion claiming his territory. Her clit throbbed. He could probably make her come just by making those sounds.

"I want to see you too." She gripped the counter, twitching as he continued tracing the edge of her panties, barely slipping his finger beneath the elastic.

"Not now."

"But…"

"Quiet."

The implacable tone of his voice silenced her. She wasn't certain how she felt about that. As much as she'd been after him, she hadn't known, not really, if she could handle the dominance and rigidity that were such an intrinsic part of him.

In theory, those qualities were one of the reasons she was so attracted to him, but she hadn't considered what it would be like to contend with them in reality.

Now she was about to find out, and her entire being tingled with a riotous combination of nervousness, disbelief, and an excitement unlike any she'd ever felt before.

Gavin slid his hands back up to cup her breasts, flicking his thumbs over her nipples. Aside from his hard breathing and the massive bulge pressing against his fly, he was still totally in control of himself.

Unlike Mia, whose tenuous control began to slip away like

raindrops falling down a windowpane. She shifted to press her breasts into his palms, mesmerized by the sight of his big, tanned hands against her pale skin, his long fingers twisting her nipples so expertly that currents of heat flowed to her core.

"God, Gavin," she whispered, flexing and unflexing her fingers on the counter's edge. "That feels so good."

A smile tugged at his mouth. "So do you."

He stroked his hands over her belly and hooked his fingers into the waistband of her panties. Mia's breath stuck in her throat as he pulled them slowly over her hips and halfway down her thighs, revealing her smooth vulva and the wet evidence of her arousal. He slipped one finger over her mons and into her cleft.

"Fucking perfect," he whispered, his voice guttural and rough.

She shuddered, arching her back to encourage his deeper penetration. "Gavin, I…"

"Do you want to come, little girl?"

She curled one hand around his rock-hard biceps, trying to stay upright. "Yes."

"Yes what?"

"Yes, *please*…oh!"

He pushed his finger into her opening, circling his thumb around her clit. Urgency burst over her veins. She tightened her grip on him, lightheadedness sweeping through her. He wrapped one arm around her waist, hauling her against him, his other hand still working her sex with expert precision.

She closed her eyes, turning her face into his chest. His heart hammered, the thump echoing into her bones. Her body vibrated with the need for release. She couldn't believe this was happening, that after all this time, Gavin Knight was holding her and touching her like this.

Her arousal coiled tighter and tighter, pulling her upward. He was saying something, his voice a low reverberation in his chest, but she couldn't make out the sound of his words. He lowered his head to her ear. His hot breath brushed the side of her neck, sending tingles racing down her spine.

"Come on, my little flirt," he whispered roughly. "You think I haven't noticed you all these months? Your perfect tits under those tight sweaters you wear. Your hard nipples. The way you cross your legs and wiggle around in your chair. Are you thinking dirty thoughts when do you that? Getting wet? You don't know how many times I've imagined bending you over a table and spreading your legs. Easing my dick into your sweet pussy, nice and slow, before fucking you hard. Hearing you moan and beg before you come with a scream."

Holy shit.

She couldn't take it. She circled her hips, silently pleading with him to increase the pressure and send her careening into bliss. He did, thrusting his fingers into her while simultaneously rubbing her clit.

"Gavin...I'm...oh!"

Her body went up in flames. She gripped him hard, squeezing her eyes shut as overwhelming sensations cascaded through her. His voice shifted to a murmur, his one hand easing the lingering vibrations from her and the other splayed firmly against her back. She shook and moaned, suffused in an exquisite pleasure that she never wanted to end. He held her through it, his arms a velvet-and-steel circle of protection.

Mia drew in a ragged breath. Awareness came back to her slowly. Aside from her open robe and the panties tangled around her thighs, she was naked and still trembling.

In Gavin Knight's arms.

His shirtfront was damp with his sweat against her cheek, his erection pushing into her belly. Even through his trousers, she felt the hot throb of his shaft, could only imagine letting him slide that massive length into her.

She shivered, her pussy clenching. Was he going to—

He pulled her robe back over her shoulders and fastened the belt. Mia stepped away, sudden heat rising to her cheeks.

Aside from the burn in his eyes, Gavin's expression revealed little of own arousal. He bent, sliding her panties down her legs.

Mia stepped out of them, bracing her hand on his shoulder. He gathered the pink panties in his fist and straightened. She held out her hand for them. Amusement glinted in his eyes before he stuffed her panties into his trouser pocket.

She stared at him. "You...you're keeping my panties?"

"Mmm." He walked to the table and began packing up his laptop.

"That's a little creepy."

He shrugged. "Do you want them back?"

She didn't, actually. The thought of her panties tucked away in his pocket made her feel warm, cozy, and dirty all at the same time.

"No," she admitted. "Just don't tell anyone you have them."

"I never kiss and tell." He closed his briefcase. "If you're bringing the binders to Wild Child tomorrow, I'll pick them up to make copies."

"You're leaving?"

"I am."

"But..." Her gaze skittered to his erection, which was only a tad less prominent than it had been. He was really going to leave all jacked up?

He picked up his briefcase and laptop.

Apparently so.

"I need to finish the reassessment by the end of the week so I can implement all extra measures and contingencies," he said.

God. Even after what he'd just done to her, he could turn back into security boss extraordinaire in the blink of an eye. She swallowed, smothering a rush of confusion and longing.

"Okay," she said. "I stop by the bakery after work, so I'm usually there around three."

"I know."

He winked at her, unsmiling, and walked out the door.

CHAPTER 5

*C*urses split through Gavin's head. He could still hear her breathy sighs, smell her scent on his fingers, feel her body trembling in his arms. He could still taste her, chocolate chips and caramel. Her pink underwear burned a hole in his pocket.

He pulled his black SUV into the driveway and went inside. The modern, wood-and-stucco house, isolated on a plot of land at the Santa Cruz foothills, usually had a calming effect on him. Not tonight. He left his briefcase by the door and poured himself a glass of scotch.

Then another.

He could start up with her. Easy as slipping thread from the eye of a needle. She was hot, willing, and ready. Her body was addictive, smooth and tight. Mia was everything he craved but hadn't had in too long. She smelled like a goddamned flower garden. He wanted to get her dirty and messy. Her voice alone made him hard.

But under her sexy, flirty manner, she was sweet. Young. She liked girly stuff—potpourri, makeup, fairies, pretty dresses, scented candles, pink and purple lace. She wanted to have fun. She loved her friends fiercely.

He'd fucking ruin her.

He took her panties from his pocket and tossed them on his bedside table. As he got into the shower, he imagined her spread out naked in front of him. Wearing the panties, so he could pull them aside while he pushed into her. She'd been so tight around his fingers. Sinking his dick into her would be heaven.

He jerked off with the images blazing in his brain. Shot all over the shower wall while picturing her smooth cunt dripping with his come. He rested his forehead against the wall, his chest heaving and his hand still fisted around his cock.

Maybe now he was tired enough to sleep okay tonight.

Instead he lay awake for a long time, staring at the ceiling and thinking of old fairy tales about spinning straw into gold, poison apples, sleeping princesses, and magic spells.

He woke after a restless sleep that—at least—hadn't been punctured by flashback nightmares. The symptoms of his PTSD had improved over the years, but sleep remained elusive and broken.

Since he'd be meeting with Luke and Warren Stone that morning, he dressed in a suit and tie. When he was installing security systems or working out of the office, he wore the Knight Security uniform of a black shirt and pants, but for consultations and meetings, even with the Stones, he preferred the suit.

As he returned to the bedroom for his cufflinks, his gaze fell on the crumpled pink panties on the nightstand. After a second's hesitation—and a thousand misgivings—he stuffed them into his jacket pocket and left the house.

He drove to the headquarters of the Sugar Rush Candy Company, assessing that the security guards were following required protocol, and that the gates and barriers worked to ensure access control.

"Anything unusual?" he asked the guard at the gate.

"No, sir. We had one visitor who wasn't on the authorized list, but he left when we denied him entry. Said he needed to talk to Evan Stone about the wedding."

Gavin frowned. "Why Evan?"

"Don't know, sir. Evan Stone isn't even on-site today, so we couldn't call up and ask him." The guard checked his tablet. "Name was Brian Hurst."

"All right, thanks."

Gavin typed a quick text to Evan asking him to call before walking to the main office. Several Knight Security operatives patrolled the grounds unobtrusively—a new guard team Gavin had ordered last week in light of the increased threat to the Stone family. He'd implemented every single security measure on the campus, as well as at the Stones' private residences and those of many of the company's employees.

At regular intervals, he double-checked that everything worked as it should. Nothing was more important to him than ensuring the safety of the people who trusted him to provide protection.

He walked to Luke's office, where his friend was waiting with Warren Stone. After greeting each other, they sat around a table in a seating area of Luke's office. Gavin took a file of copied letters out of his briefcase and handed them to Luke.

"This makes a total of twenty since the news of the wedding went public," he said. "One more arrived yesterday, and I brought the original to the police to keep with the others. He's escalating his threats, which is typical of a stalker who is trying to incite a response."

Luke and Warren scanned the letter, their foreheads creased with frowns. Gavin had already memorized the black, scrawled writing and dire threats:

I'll fucking rip your head off, Stone, you lying, motherfucking thief. You'll never live "happily ever after," you shithead.

I'm fucking bombing your goddamned wedding. You can't stop me. Body parts will fly.

You won't know the meaning of "red wedding" until your big fucking day.

Warren set the letter down, his jaw tight. "How credible is this?"

"Any threat to cause bodily harm is one to be taken seriously. The fact that he hasn't called or tried any other means of contact except for letters indicates he might not have the means to carry out the threat. However, I will make no assumptions. In my mind, this is cause for locking down the wedding venue to the securest and least obtrusive extent possible."

"Do whatever you need to do," Luke said. "I'll talk to Polly, but I won't tell her the details. She needs to be aware, not scared."

Gavin put the letter back in his briefcase. "Have you thought of anything else that might be helpful? Anyone else who was involved in the production of the Zigzag Candy?"

Luke shook his head. "You have all the records. We came up with the concept of zigzag-shaped candy in-house. R&D spent three years developing the prototype and full product line. I didn't steal the idea from anyone, much less a random nutjob who's now demanding millions in compensation."

"I know you didn't steal the idea, but I'm trying to determine why he thinks you did," Gavin explained. "If he's a disgruntled former employee, he might have contributed to the product line in some way and believes he was responsible for it."

"You have all the employee records and lists of who was involved." Luke rubbed the back of his neck. "Did the investigations turn up anything?"

"Not yet." Aside from the threatening letters, Gavin didn't have much else to go on. Because Sugar Rush treated its employees so well, the company had a very low turnover rate. The employees who had left, even some of those who'd been fired, still spoke highly, or at least respectfully, of the company.

Of course that didn't mean people weren't disgruntled with either Sugar Rush or the Stones. Luke had battled a nasty paternity suit a few years ago brought on by a vindictive ex-girlfriend, and the company's legal department worked hard to mitigate potential litigation. The majority of Gavin's job was centered on providing security for both the company and family.

This threat, however, was the most sinister yet.

"The less people know about this, the better," he said. "I've intensified security around the campus, but it shouldn't be too evident."

"What about the bakery?" Warren asked.

"I have two men stationed there 24/7," Gavin assured him. "Polly knows there's a need for tighter security because the wedding is so high profile."

"She doesn't like the idea of extra security at the bakery," Luke told his father. "But she's dealing with it."

"My men are trained to be inconspicuous." Gavin closed his briefcase. "To anyone else, they look like regular customers. I stop by both locations at least twice a day."

He stood and extended his hand. "Good to see you both. I'll be in touch."

"Hey, we're having a barbeque at Dad's house this weekend." Luke also got to his feet. "Kind of a pre-wedding party, just family and close friends. Come and join us. Starts at five on Saturday."

"Thanks. I'll check my schedule."

Luke nodded, his expression changing to a frown. They both knew that meant *"Thanks, but no thanks."* Though Gavin had practically grown up with the Stone brothers, and despite repeated invitations, he hadn't socialized with them since returning from Iraq five years ago. Aside from a few affairs with women who ended up wanting more from him than he could give, he hadn't socialized at all.

He returned to the parking lot, pausing when his phone buzzed.

"Hey, Gavin, it's Evan. You wanted to ask me about someone who showed up at Sugar Rush?"

"Yeah, said he wanted to talk to you about the wedding. Brian Hurst."

"Rings no bells. Did he say what he wanted?"

"No. Security turned him away because he wasn't authorized. He hasn't called you?"

"No, but I haven't checked my Sugar Rush messages. I don't know why he'd want to talk to me about the wedding. You want me to call you, if he left a message?"

"Yes, any time of day or night."

"Will do. You going to Dad's on Saturday?"

"No, can't make it. Thanks for calling."

He ended the call and put his phone back into his pocket. He returned to the Knight Security offices, a glass-and-steel building on the outskirts of Indigo Bay. Several of his security operatives worked with different clients, but Gavin had dedicated most of his team, as well as himself, to both the Stones and Sugar Rush.

He ran a check on Brian Hurst, which turned up the information that he'd attended the same university as Luke and owned a fireworks import and display company. On the surface, there was nothing suspicious about the guy, but Gavin would take no chances.

After working through lunch, he found himself glancing at the clock as it inched toward three. He told himself he was impatient only because he hadn't stopped at Wild Child yet that day. Not because he had Mia's underwear in his pocket and couldn't stop thinking of her sweet, hot body.

He shook his head with a humorless laugh. He was a fucking idiot. Touching her last night had been like the first hit of a drug, one he now craved more and more.

But it didn't matter if he couldn't detach himself from her. Soon enough, he'd scare her away.

CHAPTER 6

*G*avin drove to the Indigo Bay branch of Wild Child, where several customers sat at the round tables. His men were at two separate tables, one close to the door and the other near the counter. Both were alert and vigilant, despite the empty coffee mugs and plates in front of them.

One assessing sweep of the interior told him Mia wasn't there. Not that he needed to assess anything. It had gotten to the point that he *felt* her presence or absence the second he stepped into the bakery. Instinctively, he was either pleased or vaguely disappointed—and both emotions were directly tied to a pretty blonde princess.

He exchanged nods of greeting with his men before taking an empty table.

"Hi, Gavin." Polly approached, wiping her hands on her apron. "Can I get you a Declair or a croissant?"

"Not today, thanks."

Though he always declined, she still always asked. He'd tried the Declairs when Polly was first inventing the recipe, but he didn't often have one when he was at the bakery.

"I'll just have a black coffee, no sugar," he said.

"Coming right up." She gave him her friendly smile, but he detected the faint concern in her eyes, the lines of stress around her mouth.

Shit. Like Luke, the last thing Gavin wanted was for Polly to worry about the safety of her friends and family—especially right before her wedding.

"Hey." He put his hand on her arm. "I won't let anything happen to you or anyone else."

She smiled again. "I know. It's just weird stuff to deal with when all I care about is being married to Luke. Well, and for everyone to have a great time. I've dreamed of a big, happy wedding since I was a little girl, but of course I never expected to need all sorts of security."

"You'll have a big, happy wedding," Gavin assured her. "My team and any additional security will be barely noticeable. All you need to do is focus on marrying Luke and enjoying yourself. Everyone will stay safe and have a great time."

"That's the only wedding present I really want."

"You'll have it. I promise."

"Thank you." Polly squeezed his hand before glancing past him. Gavin's body went into full alert, his senses tingling even before Polly said, "Hi, Mia," and stepped away from him.

"Hey, Pols." Her voice spilled into the air like music. "I need you to pick out new ribbons for the favors. The supplier doesn't have enough for the extra ones. Here are the samples."

Polly took the folder, and they consulted for a moment.

"Mia's special caramel mochaccino?" Polly asked, heading back to the counter.

"Extra whipped cream, as usual," Mia replied. "To go."

Then she moved into his line of vision. Blond hair caught in a high ponytail. Tight purple shirt. Polka-dot mini skirt. White tights.

Instant hard-on.

"Hi." She stepped closer, her voice uncertain. "I have all the binders in the car."

"I need them to make copies."

"You can't keep them." She eased into the chair across from him. "I don't want them out of my sight. They're too important."

"You can come with me." He studied her, not liking the faint purplish smudges under her eyes. "You didn't sleep well."

She shrugged, shifting in her chair and glancing around. Then she leaned closer and whispered, "Well, you left me in quite a state."

His mouth twitched. He liked her forthrightness and honesty. He might even have liked the fact that she was making him smile more often.

"You want me to make it up to you?" he asked.

A flush rose to her cheeks before she said, "Yes."

Christ. His dick throbbed. Served him right. For all his self-censure about starting up with her, he wouldn't be able to help himself. She was too tempting, too sweet, too willing...and it had been too fucking long since he'd experienced anything close to what Mia Donovan could offer him.

If he ever had. Her bright, happy world with its heart-shaped pillows and ice cream would shine a welcome light on his darkness, if only temporarily.

He'd known that for the past year. But now that he'd had a taste of her whipped-cream lightness...

He stood and took out his wallet, dropping a few bills on the table to pay for his untouched coffee.

"Let's go," he told Mia.

After getting her takeout dessert drink—no way would he call that concoction *coffee*—Mia walked to the door. He pulled it open and stepped aside to let her exit in front of him. His gaze drifted to her ass encased in the short skirt. He wanted to flip her skirt up, pull her tights down, and—

"I'm parked over here." She walked to an old Toyota sitting at the curb. A pair of pink fuzzy dice dangled from the rearview mirror, and a UC Santa Barbara sticker decorated the bumper.

"When did you graduate?" he asked, nodding at the sticker.

"Two years ago." She set the coffee on the roof and hefted a stack of binders from the trunk. "I moved back here when I couldn't find a job.'"

"Polly told me you were working at a florist's." He took the heavy binders from her.

"They shut down a while ago." Her mouth twisted. "I work at an insurance company now."

"As an agent?"

"No. I sit in a windowless cubicle and collate reports." She slammed the trunk, collected her coffee, and fell into step beside him. "Sometimes I even staple them together. If there's ever a contest for the world's most boring job, I'm pretty sure I'm a number one contender."

"Why do you stay?"

"Because I'm a French lit major who got through all four years on a full scholarship, thereby eliminating my need to work and gain valuable career skills." A bitter note threaded her voice. "So while I can talk endlessly about Renaissance France or the politics of Proust, I have very little actual job experience. Imagine my surprise when I discovered employers don't care a whit about feminism in medieval French epics."

Gavin stopped. She took two steps before realizing he was no longer beside her. She turned, a frown pulling her eyebrows together.

"What?" she asked.

"You're being petulant," he said.

Mia stared at him before giving a short laugh. "I'm being *petulant*? Are you serious?"

"Yes. You can get discouraged, even upset, when you hit wall after wall. Which it sounds like you've done. But sulking about the fact that employers need to hire people with practical skills will do nothing to change your situation."

"Good lord, Gavin." Mia shook her head in disbelief. "You're a freaking robot, aren't you?"

"As you discovered last night..." he noted the telling blush rising to her cheeks "...I'm not a robot. And graduating from college after four years on a full scholarship is no small feat. But it doesn't mean you're allowed to be bitter when Fortune 500 companies aren't fighting to hire you."

"I don't want to work for a Fortune 500 company," Mia snapped. "But I don't want to work in a cubicle at an insurance company either."

"So what do you want to do?"

"I don't know!" She threw one hand up in the air, her body tensing with frustration. "That's the problem. As far as skills go, mine are limited to writing academic papers, speaking French, and having fun. If you have any job openings I might fit, then by all means, let me know."

"That's not what I asked you," Gavin said. "I asked what you *want* to do."

"I..." Mia's mouth opened and closed. She stepped back, her hands balling into fists. "I don't know."

She glared daggers at him and stalked away, her back rigid. He caught up with her.

"You can get mad at me," he said. "I can take it. Blame me for forcing you to confront something you don't want to face. But I won't let you hide from the truth."

"Oh, shut up," Mia retorted. "Were you a therapist in a previous life or something?"

"No, but I've been in a lot of therapy."

Some of the anger drained from her, replaced with curiosity. "Really? You've been in therapy?"

He nodded. "After my sixth tour in Iraq. I was given an

honorable discharge for medical reasons, one of which was PTSD."

"Oh." Her voice sounded smaller. "I'm sorry. I didn't know."

Gavin stopped by his SUV, put the binders in the back seat, and opened the passenger side door for her. She ducked her head as she started to pass him. He slipped his hand beneath her chin, turning her face toward him. Wariness flooded her green eyes along with a hint of shame. He brushed his thumb over her lips.

"What I or anyone else has experienced doesn't change things for you," he said. "It doesn't mean you can't want more than what you have. It doesn't mean you don't deserve more."

She only looked at him. The sun glinted off her hair like a halo. Little angel with her silly flirting, her boring insurance job, and her frilly, feminine apartment.

"You're…" Her lips moved against his thumb, her breath warm. "You're the strangest man I've ever met, Gavin Knight."

He leaned closer, brushing a kiss close to her ear. "But I can make you come so hard you'll see stars."

She drew in a sharp breath. A visible shiver ran through her.

"Prove it," she whispered.

Damned if he didn't love her little challenges. And at that second, there was nothing he wanted to do more than *prove it*.

"I will." He forced himself to step back and motioned for her to get into the SUV. "But first we have copies to make."

She gave a little harrumph of annoyance before climbing into the passenger seat. Gavin drove back to the Knight Security offices, where he and Mia systematically took apart the wedding plan binders and made copies of all the relevant pages. He locked the copies in his office safe before they returned to the SUV.

"Can I see your place?" Mia pulled the seat belt over her body.

He glanced at her. "Do you usually ask to go to a man's house?"

"No. And I'm not a slut, if that's what you're thinking."

"That's not what I'm thinking."

"I like to flirt and go out and stuff, but I don't sleep around casually," Mia continued. "The last boy I slept with…we'd been dating exclusively for three months."

He blocked the thought of her with a "boy."

"Why are you telling me this?" he asked.

"I don't want you to judge me."

He shifted into drive. "Do you think I would?"

"Sometimes. When you wouldn't pay attention to me, I figured you were thinking I was just this flirty little girl who wasn't worth your time."

"You are a flirty little girl." He shot her a half-grin. "But you're definitely worth my time."

A responding smile curved her mouth. He was tempted to drive her to her apartment—he wanted to be back in the place that had *her* stamped all over it—but he had a stronger urge to see her in his bed. And to cook her dinner.

He drove back to his house. Mia peered out the front windshield as he turned onto the narrow road leading to the hillside grove.

"This is really pretty," she remarked. "It's like one of those houses designed to blend in with the environment."

"Most women think it's too austere."

"I imagine most women think *you're* too austere," she said dryly.

He almost laughed. It wouldn't take her long to figure out that was the truth. Hell, he was counting on her walking away from his austerity. She'd leave a trail of ribbons and rose petals in her wake.

He unlocked the front door and pushed it open, waiting for her to precede him. She went inside, looking around at the neutral furnishings, the bamboo plants, the black-and-white prints.

"Very Zen." She ran her hand over the teakwood sideboard. "So do you bring a lot of women here?"

Though her voice was casual, a faint tension threaded her frame. Gavin tossed his keys on the table and shook his head.

"I haven't brought a woman here in a while."

"When was the last time you had a girlfriend?"

"Probably when I was in college." He walked into the kitchen. "I'm inclined toward short-term relationships. Or no relationship at all."

Her expression darkened. A warning sign flashed in his brain. He'd crossed the line of their attraction, but he couldn't let her get any ideas about a *relationship*. She was all about romance and pretty things. He was neither.

He gave her a level look. "You need to know that."

"What, that you're a stodgy old stick-in-the-mud who's forgotten what it feels like to loosen up?" She lifted her eyebrows in mock surprise. "Guess what? I already knew that."

Gavin suppressed a smile. "And yet it didn't stop you."

"Because I'm the one who's meant to help you loosen up." She leaned against the kitchen doorjamb, her arms crossed. Against the gray and olive-green colors of his house, she looked like a flower in her purple shirt and polka-dot skirt.

No, he couldn't stay away from her any longer. He'd spent a year withstanding the hot pull of Mia Donovan. Now she was proving far too addicting even for his hardened self-discipline.

He turned away from her and opened the refrigerator. He took out a package of ribeye steaks, along with tomatoes, green beans, kale, and potatoes.

"Are you making dinner?" Mia asked.

"I am."

"That looks impressive." She moved closer almost tentatively, as if she wasn't sure if he'd appreciate her entering his space. "Can I help?"

"Sure. Knives are over there. You can cube the potatoes."

She washed her hands and set to work while he heated pans on the gas stove and seasoned the steaks. Soon the kitchen was filled with the aromas of grilled steaks and roasting vegetables.

Gavin uncorked a bottle of wine and poured a glass for her before getting his usual scotch.

"So did you start Knight Security after you came back from Iraq?" Mia asked.

He nodded. "I'd worked in security before that, but wanted to start my own business. Luke was looking to revamp the Sugar Rush security, both physical and cyber, so I took the job."

"You were friends with Luke before?"

"I've known him since we were kids."

"Like me and Polly." Mia hitched herself onto a stool at the central island. "We met in fourth grade after she and her mom moved to Rainsville to open Wild Child."

"So you grew up here?"

"Born and bred. Aside from living in Santa Barbara during college, I've stuck to the Indigo Bay area. My parents divorced when I was fifteen and moved to different parts of the country, so I went to live with my granny down by the beach."

He liked the fairy-tale quality of that picture. Mia and Granny, living in a ramshackle little cottage on the beach.

"Does your grandmother still live here?" he asked.

Sorrow tightened her features. "She died right after my senior year of college. I moved back to take care of things and...well, I never left."

"Do you want to leave?"

"Not at all." Mia traced the edge of her glass with her finger. "I love Indigo Bay. I just want to be doing something different, more fulfilling. My granny was an artist, so she had this vision that we should make the world beautiful, whether through paintings or planting flowers or helping others. She always told me to follow my heart, do what I love and love what I do. I guess I'm still figuring out what that is."

An unexpected tenderness nudged at Gavin. Mia Donovan

was a girl who made the world more beautiful just by living in it. But she used her flirty, flaunting ways to hide her guilt because she hadn't yet followed her granny's advice.

This girl was turning out to be more of a surprise than he'd anticipated. And he wasn't supposed to *like* surprises.

He turned to the stove and checked the steaks. He took two plates from the cupboard and loaded them with the steak, vegetables, and potatoes. After setting one in front of Mia, he sat beside her at the counter.

She bit into her steak and murmured a noise of approval that flickered right into his blood.

"Wow, you're a really good cook," she said. "This is delicious."

He took an inordinate amount of pleasure in her appreciation, as well as the fact that she ate with gusto.

"So why the military?" She sliced into a potato.

"My father was a retired Marine corporal. A tough one. It was drilled into me early on that I'd join the Marines. Never thought there was an option."

She glanced at him. "But you didn't want to?"

"I knew I'd be good at it. By the time I was twelve, I'd been smacked around and ridden hard enough that I figured I could get through anything."

She stilled, her gaze on him. "Your father was abusive."

Gavin shrugged. "He eased up when I hit my teens and got bigger than him. Took a knockdown, drag-out fight to warn him he couldn't fuck with me anymore. But it worked."

"What happened to him?"

"He died ten years ago. Heart attack."

Mia fell silent, looking down at her food. He felt the distress simmering inside her. He didn't like it, didn't like making her feel anything unpleasant, but he'd meant what he'd said to her earlier. He wouldn't let her hide from the truth. Not even his.

He pushed his plate away. She'd stopped eating and was rubbing her thumb over the edge of her wineglass. Her fingers were long and tapered, the nails painted a glossy pink with silver glitter. He imagined her sitting on her sofa, a romantic comedy playing on the TV. Her head bent, long hair falling forward as she carefully painted her nails.

Gavin turned both their stools so they were facing each other. She fixed her gaze on his shirtfront, her eyes downcast. He rubbed a few loose strands of her hair between his fingers and tucked them behind her ear.

"The Stone brothers were my safe house," he said. "They never knew how bad it was, not even Luke, but their family treated me like one of their own. If there was anything I wished for when I was a kid, it was to have been born into that family. To be one of them. They stayed in contact whenever I was deployed. Letters, care packages, video calls. Kept me sane."

She lifted her gaze to his. Her green eyes seared right through him.

"Were you in Iraq for all six tours?"

"Yes."

"What was it like?" she asked. "If you want to talk about it."

He didn't—not because he hadn't dealt with it, but because he hated the idea of it tainting her.

Multiple kills. Not always insurgents. The bombs that blew apart his fellow soldiers. Hauling body parts into the Humvee so no one would get left behind. Stench of rust, blood, and gun smoke that still permeated his nightmares. Heat and dirt. A girl's foot, clad in a yellow plastic sandal, lying by the side of the road.

Any woman he was with had to learn about all that eventually —which was one reason he always cut his relationships short. If a woman wasn't there, she didn't have to know.

But Mia...she had to know. Sooner rather than later, so she'd run away from him back to the safety of her princess tower.

What was it like?

"You know the expression *war is hell*?" he said.

She nodded.

"That's not what it's like. That's what it is." He didn't take his gaze from hers, needing her to see the darkness discoloring his life. "A twenty-year-old kid on his first tour fires ten rounds of ammunition into a car, thinking it's a suicide bomber. Turns out he just killed a family of five. On a convoy, a grenade hits the truck ahead of his, and he can't save the soldiers trapped under the vehicle. He loses track of the number of IEDs exploding around him, killing his comrades. Figures one day it'll be his turn."

The shock and despair in her eyes stabbed right through him.

"My god, Gavin." Mia put her hand on his chest, the warmth of her palm sinking right into him. "You keep all that in here?"

His past was no longer a fire, hot and burning. It had died down to ashes that still smoldered, but could at least be controlled. And Mia was like a rush of cool, clear water pouring right down his parched throat.

He was so fucking greedy for more.

Her ponytail was draped over her shoulder like a gold ribbon. He twisted it around his fist and tugged, pulling her closer. Her lips parted the instant before he crushed his mouth to hers.

CHAPTER 7

She was falling again, the galaxy of stars spread like a velvet blanket around her. Except this time, she would land right in the arms of this strong, complicated man who made her heart hurt and her body burn.

He slipped his hands to the sides of her neck, deepening the kiss. She curled her fists into his shirtfront, already lightheaded with blissful sensations. The taste of him—scotch and pure maleness—lit her blood on fire.

He moved off the stool without breaking the contact of their mouths. Took hold of her waist and lifted her right against him, as if she weighted no more than a feather. She obeyed the unspoken command and wrapped her legs around his waist and her arms around his neck.

He curved his large hands down to her bottom, holding her in place as he strode out of the kitchen. Mia was so awash in pleasure that she didn't notice until he lifted his head that they were in his bedroom.

Her heart hammered, excitement and a hint of trepidation rising inside her. Much as she'd teased him, she wasn't at all certain she could actually take everything he could, and would, give her. He was worlds apart from the college boys she'd been with—a hard, wounded, disciplined solider whose innate sense of command permeated all parts of his life.

He lowered her slowly, letting her body slide against his. Her nipples stiffened, her thighs trembling. His breath escaped as he pulled her shirt over her head, revealing the purple lace bra that pushed her breasts into a generous valley of cleavage. She thought for sure he would take her skirt off next, but instead he turned her around so her back was to him.

His breath brushed her nape. His body was a solid wall behind her, his erection shoving against her lower back. He placed his hand flat on her midriff and worked it under her skirt and tights, right into her cleft.

Mia gasped, arching into his touch. He took her other hand and guided it to his groin. Arousal flared through her. She palmed the heavy, thick ridge of his erection, following it to where it rested along his thigh. *Good god.*

"On the bed." His voice was a low, guttural order that Mia couldn't have disobeyed if she'd tried.

Which she didn't.

She climbed onto the bed, goosebumps prickling her skin. Before she could turn back around, he slid his hands to her thighs, parting them. She twisted to look at him over her shoulder, her breath catching at his expression—severe and unreadable save for the lust burning deep and dark in his blue eyes.

He motioned with his forefinger for her to turn again. She did, grabbing a pillow because she had a feeling she would need something to hold on to. Gavin stroked his hands over her legs, pausing to trace the flowers on her tights with his fingers. Then he flipped her skirt up and rubbed her bottom, the heat of his large palm burning through her tights and underwear.

He grasped the waistband of her tights and panties. She squeezed her eyes shut as he yanked them down, baring her ass and the cleft of her pussy, which she knew was already shiny with arousal. She buried her face in the pillow, a blush rising hot to her cheeks at the sudden, shocking realization that Gavin Knight—the man she'd teased relentlessly for a year—was now gazing at her private parts.

For all her flirtations and fantasies, she hadn't considered what it would feel like to actually be exposed to this battle-hardened man who had a wealth of experience over her. Turned out it was thrilling, wildly exciting, and a little scary all at the same time.

Gavin slipped his finger between her legs, stroking up and down, teasing her clit. She groaned, gripping the pillow tighter, unable to fully open for him out of both shyness and the fact that her tights were still laced around her thighs. She twisted toward him again, but he placed his hand on her back to indicate that she should remain still.

He ran his fingertips up and down her thighs, creating a tickling pleasure over her skin. She squirmed, heat pooling in her lower body. He made no sound aside from the increased weight of his breathing.

"Gavin, please."

He stroked her bare bottom in response, then gave it a light spank that sent a thrill through her. The unmistakable sounds of his shirt falling to the floor and his zipper rasping open as he shed his clothes jolted Mia's heart. She struggled not to turn around, aching though she was to finally see Gavin's body.

He moved away from her for an instant and tucked another pillow beneath her hips. A condom packet ripped open. Her body tensed with both nerves and excitement. Though in all her fantasies, he'd always taken her from the front—at least, at first— he appeared to have a different plan in mind.

Clutching her hips, he tugged her farther down the bed and nudged her legs apart wider. The elastic of her tights dug into her thighs. He worked his finger into her cleft again, a low chuckle rumbling from his throat when he discovered just how wet and ready she was.

"Gavin..." She panted, wiggling her hips a little in invitation. "Fuck me."

"Bad words from such a pretty mouth." He gave her bottom another slap—hard enough to sting but not really hurt. "Spread your legs as wide as you can, honey."

Pulse pounding, she did, though her thighs trembled from the constriction of the tights. His breath sawed through the air, heavy and deep. Then the head of his cock pressed against her damp slit.

She gasped and arched forward, her head spinning. She'd known he was big, but she hadn't imagined he'd feel *impossibly* big, like there was no way he'd ever fit inside her.

He stopped, his hands tight on her ass. "Don't tense up."

Mia took a breath, flexing and unflexing her fists on the pillow. He slipped his fingers inside her, opening her even more. A sudden heat flushed over her as she imagined what she must look like, her skirt flipped over her back, her tights still around her thighs, and her body spread open on display.

For *him.*

She pressed her face in the pillow. He pushed forward, penetrating her inch by inch, his thick shaft stretching her fully.

"Ah, *fuck.*" His deep groan reverberated through her blood.

Sweat broke out on her skin. Her body worked to accommodate him, the heat of his cock pulsing inside her. Gradually her trepidation eased, colored over with a pleasure that mounted with every powerful beat of her heart.

He stilled, fully seated inside her, his voice strained. "Okay?"

She nodded, unable to speak past the warmth in her throat. Electric sparks shot over her nerves. He moved his hands to her waist, steadying her. Then he started to move, easing partway out of her before rocking forward. The gentle movement allayed the last of her anxiety, as he primed her to accept his rhythm.

Her breath burned her chest. She stretched her arms out, grasping the sheets, her nipples chafing on the bedcover. He increased his rhythm slowly but steadily, his hair-roughened thighs abrading hers, his fingers digging into her hips. Her clit throbbed, the constraint of her tights increasing the delicious pressure.

"Gavin..." His name escaped on a rush of air. "That's so good...please..."

He slipped one hand beneath her, his fingers finding the swollen bud. "Come on, my sweet little princess. Nice and hard."

Mia gave up all pretense of control and writhed beneath him, pushing back to meet his thrusts. Her body jolted against the bed, his cock driving her arousal higher and higher. She whimpered and moaned, struggling with the need for release and the overwhelming urge for this intense bliss to go on and on forever.

"Gavin, I feel it," she gasped, her fever rising to the breaking point. "I'm so close, I—"

He pulled out of her abruptly. Confusion flooded her for half an instant before he grabbed her hips and turned her to face him.

Mia stared at him through the veil of hair that had fallen over her face. Need blazed in his blue eyes, sweat trickled down his temple, and his jaw was set with restraint.

And his *body*...more gorgeous and powerful than she could have imagined, with sculpted pecs and a rigid washboard abdomen that she wanted to touch all over. His sheathed cock stood straight out from his groin, pulsing almost visibly, damp with her fluids.

Without hesitation, she pushed her panties and tights off, unzipped her skirt, and moved back on the bed, spreading her legs wide. A growl rumbled in his chest. He mounted her, shoving his hands under her thighs and plunging into her. She gripped his arms, unable to take her eyes off his, struck to the core by the hot, crackling energy that bound them together.

She came with a cry, arching up against him, stars exploding behind her eyes. Even as the sensations consumed her, he kept moving, fitting them together again and again, letting her rise and fall through the wave. Only when her pleasure began to ebb did he loosen the reins of his control. He sank deep inside her with a rough shout, his muscles locking and tensing beautifully as he surrendered to his own release.

He rolled beside her on the bed, his chest heaving. Mia fell back against the pillows and pressed her hands to her face. Her body trembled and quivered with lingering sensations, but even through the intense physical pleasure she sensed a profound shift deep inside her, like the plates of the earth separating and coming back together.

His hand settled on her belly. Mia lowered her arms slowly and opened her eyes. She turned her head to face him, finding him watching her with a hooded gaze. She wanted to reach out and touch his face, smooth the crease from between his eyebrows, soften his rigid jaw.

Before she gave in to the urge, she fumbled to wrap the sheet around her body and climbed out of bed. She went to the bathroom, unable to help herself from looking at Gavin's personal items—the black brush on the counter, the straight-edged razor and bar of shaving soap, the prescription bottle of sleeping pills.

She returned to the bedroom and got back into bed, her insides fluttering as the scent of sex wafted over her.

"Do you want me to go?" she asked.

"No. You're staying."

The command—soft, rough, drowsy—lodged somewhere in her soul. There had once been a time when she couldn't have imagined Gavin Knight ordering her to *stay*. She'd hoped for it, maybe fantasized about it, but deep inside she'd never really believed this impassive, hardened soldier would allow her this close.

She curled up beside him, feeling as if months rather than hours had passed since he'd shown up at her doorstep yesterday.

She ran her finger over his pectoral muscles, fascinated by their sheer hardness, the strength that ran through every inch of his body.

"Do you have trouble sleeping?" She slid her hand down to his abs. "I saw the pills in the bathroom."

"Yeah." He put his arm over his eyes. "Sometimes shit comes back when my guard is down. Nightmares."

An ache filled her chest. She didn't want to imagine what he'd been through. What still haunted him. But his darkness made her, with her stuffed animals, heart-shaped pillows, and love of French romantic poetry, feel pointless and juvenile. While she'd been worrying about finding the right shade of lip gloss, Gavin had been in hell.

She turned away from him, hugging a pillow to her chest. The bed shifted. He slipped his arm around her waist and pulled her back against him. The strength of his chest and his rhythmic breathing eased a little of her distress. She rubbed her cheek on the pillow.

"I'd never hurt you," he said.

"I know." She closed her eyes. "But I hate that you went through so much bad stuff."

He was silent for a moment before he asked, "You want to know why I pretended to ignore you for so long?"

"Yes."

"Because you make the bad stuff disappear." He threaded his hand through her hair. "I go into the bakery, and you're there, like an ice-cream cone on a hot day. And I can sneak looks at you and think about how pretty you look in that skirt and about all the dirty things I want to do to you. I listen to you talk about needing a date for the weekend and planning to see some new band. I watch you bustling around, helping Polly behind the counter, decorating cupcakes. I smell your sweet scent every time you pass me. And the whole time I'm sitting there, I'm not thinking of anything except how fucking perfect the universe is to have created a girl like you."

Mia's heart skipped a thousand beats. She turned in his arms, searching his expression for the tenderness his words evoked.

She touched his jaw. "That...that's the most I've ever heard you say."

"It's the truth."

"But why did you have to ignore me to do all that?"

"I was afraid if I talked to you, I'd break the spell."

She traced his mouth with her fingers, stroking the secret notch beneath his lower lip. She couldn't imagine him being *afraid* of anything.

"And now is the spell broken?" she whispered.

"No." He curled a lock of her hair around his finger. "Now I'm trapped."

CHAPTER 8

*H*e woke from a shallow sleep, his breathing hard. Panic rustled in his chest. A few seconds passed before he realized he hadn't woken from a replay of exploding bombs and gunfire, the rancid stench of blood.

No. Instead his head was filled with the smell of vanilla and flowers, underscored by the musky odor of sex. He turned. Mia lay turned away from him, her hair spread out like a fan on the pillow, her soft body wrapped around a pillow, her bare shoulder smooth and golden. Sleeping beauty.

He looked at the clock. Five a.m. He got out of bed, tugging on a pair of shorts. He used the bathroom, brushed his teeth, and splashed cold water on his face. Mia was still asleep when he emerged.

He went into the kitchen and cleaned the pans and dishes from the previous night before starting a pot of coffee. He sat at the desk and leafed through yesterday's mail.

Instinctively, his guard went up at the sight of an envelope with his name and address written in scrawly black writing. He tore it open and pulled out a piece of paper.

Saw you on TV telling a fucking reporter about the "road closures" and "security" for the fucking wedding.

One word for you and Stone. BOOM.

Gavin set the letter and envelope aside to give to the police. The threat was one he'd heard before. But he didn't like that the stalker knew his home address. That was information he guarded fiercely.

"Morning."

He turned from his desk. Mia stood in the kitchen doorway, wearing his button-down shirt with the sleeves rolled up. The shirt fell almost to her knees. Her feet were bare, her hair a tangled mess around her shoulders. He wanted to eat her up.

"Morning. You didn't leave."

"You told me to stay." She approached, her footsteps silent on the tile floor. "Besides, you drove me here, remember? I have no way of getting home."

He grasped her hips, pulling her onto his lap. She curled against him like a warm kitten, drawing her legs up and resting her head against his shoulder.

"Now who's trapping who?" She pressed a kiss to the side of his neck.

His blood thickened. A possessive part of him did want to trap her. Keep her here all to himself, a princess in a tower. Only one key. In his pocket.

"I'll make you breakfast." He patted her thigh. "Then I need to get ready for work."

"Yeah." She sighed, her breath brushing his neck. "I should go home and change."

She eased herself off his lap. A rush of cold air filled the empty space she'd left.

"You don't have to cook anything." She poured a cup of coffee from the pot. "I'll grab something on the way to work."

"Fast food?" He shook his head and took a carton of eggs from the refrigerator. "No. This will take less than ten minutes."

She sipped the coffee and made a face. "What is this?"

"Coffee."

"*This*," she pointed at the mug, "is not coffee."

He indicated the can of ground coffee sitting beside the pot.

She took another experimental sip. "It tastes terrible."

"Sorry." Gavin cracked eggs into a bowl. Though his apology was flippant, he experienced an actual pang of regret that he couldn't offer her one of her ridiculous caramel-chocolate concoctions loaded with whipped cream and rainbow sprinkles.

"Do you have any milk and sugar?" Mia asked.

"No." But the next time she stayed over, he would. And there would definitely be a *next time*.

"Do you even eat sugar?" she asked.

"Not if I can help it. Sit down."

"You like ordering people around, don't you?"

"I like ordering you around. I also like taking care of you."

"Hmm." The noise rumbled in her throat like a purr. "I definitely like being taken care of by you. Maybe I even like it a little when you order me around."

"Then why aren't you sitting down?"

She rolled her eyes, her mouth curving with amusement, but sat at the counter. He cooked up a spinach omelet, put bread in the toaster, and sliced strawberries. A few minutes later, he piled a plate with the food and set it in front of her.

"You're really into eating healthy." She took a bite of the omelet, eyeing his chest. "And working out."

He shrugged. "I had to be strong to deal with my father. Figured out early on that working out and eating well helped me both mentally and physically."

"Is that why you're kind of on my case about it?"

"Your nutrition needs work." He eyed her chest in return, his blood heating at the sight of her breasts rounding the fabric of the shirt. "But there's not a damned thing wrong with your body."

She flashed him a smile. He could get addicted to her smile. Hell, he already was. He leaned his elbows on the counter, his hand around his coffee mug.

"I'll review all the new plans for the wedding today and implement the necessary security changes," he said in an attempt to remember his main goal. "I want to do two walkthroughs of the venue, one this week and one the day before the wedding."

"I'm meeting the caterer at the villa tomorrow at ten," Mia said. "She wants to see where she'll set up and the layout of the room."

"I'll be there."

He waited for her to finish eating before he headed back to shower, shave, and dress. Tempted though he was to bring her into the shower with him, he had work to do. Not that that made it any easier to drive her back to her car.

The morning sun burned through the gray layer of ocean fog as he drove back to Indigo Bay. He stopped at an upscale coffeehouse, telling Mia to wait in the SUV before he went inside. He returned with a lidded, cardboard cup and handed it to her.

"What's this?" She took the cup.

"Something called a caramel macchiato with chocolate syrup and extra whipped cream." Gavin started the car and headed toward downtown. "It's not your specialty drink, but the girl at the counter said it's good."

"Barista," Mia said, a smile in her voice.

"What?"

"The girl at the counter of a coffeehouse is called a *barista*."

"Well, she said it's good."

Mia pried off the lid and took a sip, then made one of those happy little noises in the back of her throat. He was starting to lov…*really like* the sounds she made.

"It's delicious," she said. "Thank you."

He shrugged off her thanks, though her smile and evident pleasure made him feel like he'd just won the lottery. He tried to smother the feeling, knowing it would lead him nowhere good, as he parked behind her car and they got out.

He put all the wedding binders back in the trunk and slammed it shut, resting his hands on the top.

"So…thanks." Mia tossed her purse into the front seat and set her coffee in the cup holder. "I mean, that was fun."

Fun. Not a word he'd have used, even if it was true. *Fun* implied a one-time thing or a date she'd have with a college boy. This wasn't a one-time thing, or even two. No fucking way.

She put her hand on the open door, shifting her weight uncertainly to one foot. For all her sassy confidence, she had spells of hesitation and self-consciousness that showed in her fidgety movements.

He suspected it was a result of her hard shift from the sheltered ivory tower of academia back to mundane reality. She'd been lauded and admired in college, which was likely also why she'd turned up her flirtations to the tenth degree after graduation. If she could no longer be admired for her academic abilities, she'd draw attention with her looks and coyness.

He approached her, sliding his hand around the back of her neck. She parted her lips in expectation of a kiss.

"I'll be finished with work around nine," he said. "Wait for me at your place."

She arched an eyebrow in challenge. "I might have plans tonight, you know."

"Cancel them."

She crossed her arms and gave him a mutinous look, as if she wanted to find out what he'd do if she resisted. And he wanted to show her, but this wasn't the time.

He narrowed his eyes sternly. "I mean it."

She grinned. "'Anybody want a peanut?'"

"What?"

Mia's expression shifted to one of disbelief. "You're kidding. Vizzini and Fezzik?"

"What are you talking about?" And how had she gotten him off-topic?

She threw up her hands in exasperation. "*The Princess Bride*. Haven't you ever seen it?"

"I don't know. Probably."

"If you had, you'd remember the rhyming," Mia said. "You'd remember everything. *To blave, you killed my father, is this a kissing book, inconceivable—*"

Gavin grasped her shoulders, hauling her against him. He planted a swift, hard kiss on her lips.

"Enough," he said. "I'll be at your place tonight. And at noon, I want you to text me a list of five things you're good at that aren't a result of your academic success. And that have nothing to do with flipping your hair or your knowledge of *The Princess Bride*."

"Five things I'm good at?" Mia blinked. "Are you serious?"

"I am."

"What for?"

He fisted his hand in her hair and gently tugged. "So we'll both know."

She gave a short laugh. "Like I said...strangest man I've ever met."

"Noon." He stepped away from her.

She got into the car, pushing the key into the ignition.

"But you were right," she admitted. "You can definitely make me come hard enough to see stars. Galaxies of them."

She tossed him a smile, flipped her hair back, and drove off. He watched her until her car rounded a corner and disappeared from sight.

ow I'm trapped.
His words reverberated back to her as she sat in her windowless cubicle, compiling and stapling reports.

That wasn't how she wanted to make him feel. It sounded as if Gavin had been trapped for most of his life—both by his father and his lack of choice in a career and his duties. Then by wartime experiences too dreadful to name, and now by his own mind and inflexibility.

No, she didn't want to trap Gavin Knight. She wanted to be the one to set him free. Being free meant being happy.

And while Mia didn't feel exactly *free* in her boring job, she had enough friends and fun times to offset the tedium and total lack of workplace socialization. The two sallow-faced insurance agents were always holed away in their own offices, so her main work relationships were with the copier and the filing cabinet.

But it wasn't as if she planned to keep the job—or be "petulant" about it—forever. She just had to figure out what to do next.

She stuck a file folder in the cabinet and turned to the blank sheet of paper on the desk.

Five things she was good at. The order had stuck in the back of her mind all morning.

She glanced at the clock. Quarter to twelve. She was half-tempted to ignore the command and not send him anything. Part of her just wanted to know what he'd do if she disobeyed. The other bigger part of her wanted to find out why he'd dreamed up this little exercise in the first place.

What was she good at that didn't have anything to do with French literature or academics? She couldn't cook. She couldn't sing or play a musical instrument. She could dance, but only in the context of a club. Math wasn't her strong suit.

She was good at fashion, makeup, and flirting, but Gavin knew that already. And she wasn't supposed to include stuff like that anyway.

She picked up the pen and wrote:

I'm good at decorating.

That was true. Her apartment was a little haven of charm, and although she didn't know if she could style a room to be modern and contemporary, that wasn't the point. Everyone had their own style and taste, and hers happened to be French Country with a crapload of girliness thrown into the mix.

She added: *I'm a good friend.*

Was that a skill? Maybe not. She crossed it off the list.

I'm good at organizing stuff.

That was because she'd collated and filed so many damned reports.

I'm good with people.

Probably that was why she was so unhappy here at Ye Olde Insurance Agency. No one to talk to. At least when she helped Polly at Wild Child, she could chat with customers and be social. People seemed to like her, too. Surely that was a good quality.

Three down. Two to go.

She tapped her pen on the desk. The fact that she had to *think* so hard about this was rather demoralizing.

I'm good at photography and making scrapbooks.

Also true. She'd created a scrapbook for her granny's seventy-fifth birthday, and she'd done several for her friends commemorating their high-school or college years. One of her wedding gifts to Polly and Luke would be a full scrapbook of their wedding, complete with photos and mementos.

She brought up Gavin's number on her phone and typed out the first four skills in a text, numbering them one to four. Then, because it was the truth, she again added *I'm a good friend.* For number six, she typed:

I'm good at making the bad stuff disappear.

She hit the send button and put her phone away. Her stomach knotted. She wanted to see him again. Badly. She really wanted to have sex with him again—because that had been more mind-blowing than anything she'd ever experienced—but she also just wanted *him.*

She wanted to curl up on his lap and feel his arms lock around her. She wanted him to bring her ice cream and call her a pretty girl. She wanted to feel his strong body beside hers as she fell asleep. She wanted to wear his shirts and smell him on her skin. She wanted him to trust her with his secrets.

She *didn't* really want him looking right into her and forcing her faults to the surface, but if that was part of having him, then so be it. If anyone could handle her faults, he could.

He could handle anything. She'd known that about him the minute she saw him. His strength was just one of the things that had drawn her to him. He could fold her right into himself, like an eagle wrapping strong wings around her.

But she had never considered that if he did that, she might not want to come out again. She might just want to lose herself in him.

She checked her phone repeatedly for the next couple of hours, but no response to her text came. Then one of the insurance agents got mad at her for misfiling a report, which made her feel worse.

"It doesn't take a genius to figure this out," he snapped at her. "Or maybe it does."

Mia barely suppressed the urge to make a face at him when he stalked back to his office. Her day went further downhill when her favorite silk scarf caught the sharp edge of a metal cabinet and ripped.

She could hardly wait to see Gavin again, wanting nothing more than to nestle into his lap and forget about all the lousy stuff. Unfortunately she had to wait until nine.

After work, she made her usual stop at Wild Child in the hopes of improving her mood. Only a few customers sat at the tables, and Polly and her sister Hannah were huddled at the counter, looking at a website displaying a vast mountain range.

"Hey, Mia." Polly straightened to give her a smile. "Caramel-chocolate mochaccino?"

"No, thanks." Mia half expected her friend to notice something was different about her. She certainly felt different.

"Polly and I are thinking of taking a trip to Kenya next year." Hannah gestured to the website. "Evan might even be able to go, if his doctor okays the trip. I was telling her about a safari I took once when I was there. Definitely a place you need to visit at least once."

Mia glanced at the website. Polly had come such a long way in the past year, not only with Luke but having reconciled with her estranged sister. Polly and Hannah had gotten quite close since Hannah had returned to Indigo Bay last summer.

Yet another change Mia had been struggling to accept.

"I stopped by to see if you wanted to come with me to happy hour at Asante," she said to Polly. "We haven't been in ages. Two for one martinis, and they're trying out some new small plates."

"Oh, I can't." Polly's forehead creased. "Luke's picking me up for a dinner thing. Maybe another night?"

"Sure." Mia glanced at Hannah, whom she liked but still resented a little for all the years she hadn't been there for Polly and their mother. "Do you want to go?"

"I can't either, sorry. I need to finish a blog post tonight. But thanks for asking."

"Sure." Mia hitched her bag over her shoulder and stepped back toward the door. "Well, I guess I'll head out then. I have my final dress fitting on Friday. Anything else you need me to do?"

"Heavens, no," Polly said. "You've done so much already. I can't thank you enough."

"You don't have to."

"You're coming to the barbeque on Saturday, right?" Polly asked. "Luke's house, around five. Don't bring anything except yourself."

"I'll be there."

Mia headed outside, texting two other friends to see if they were available. Both Anna and Susan responded that they'd meet her at the bar, which made Mia feel better. At least she didn't have to go home and sit around alone waiting for Gavin.

She took advantage of the warm evening to walk to the bar on First Street. Neither of her friends had arrived yet, so she staked out a table and ordered a lemon drop martini.

"Hi, Mia," said a male voice. "Need some company?"

She glanced up. Danny approached her, a pint of beer in his hand and a grin on his face.

"Sure." She indicated the empty seat opposite her. "The girls on are their way. Nicer place than Rave, huh?"

"Yeah, I'm celebrating because I got an interview with a sales company up in Santa Cruz." Danny pulled out the chair and sat down. "It's entry level, but has a lot of room for advancement."

"That's great. Congratulations."

"Not a done deal yet." He shrugged and took a swallow of beer. "What about you? Still planning the wedding?"

"Yes, but I have nothing on the radar after it's over," Mia

admitted. In fact, the only thing she was looking forward to after the wedding was working at Wild Child when Polly and Luke were on their honeymoon. At least her bakery shifts would break up the mundanity of her days.

"I need to start sending my resume out again," she told Danny. "I've been so busy with the wedding I haven't even kept an eye on potential jobs."

"What field are you looking at?"

"Academia, I guess." Though Mia didn't love the idea of being closed up in a library or helping a professor with research, at least she maybe she could find something that spoke to her strengths.

But was academia her strength? She loved the beauty of French literature and the language, and she'd been a dedicated student, but she hadn't envisioned having a scholarly career. Quite the contrary. Driven by the desire for a cultured life surrounded by both loveliness and excitement, she'd seen herself living in Paris, perhaps consulting with museum curators or working in foreign services.

But after Granny died, Mia had been so mired in grief that returning to Indigo Bay after graduation had been all she could manage. She'd told herself she'd get a temp job while she took the time to settle Granny's estate and mourn her loss. Once she felt strong enough again, she'd get started with her career.

Two years later, she was still stuck here and hadn't "started" anything, much less a career. Maybe she still didn't feel strong enough to make a change. Or maybe it was just that the more time passed, the harder it was to get out of the tedium of her life and routine.

Granny's edicts about "do what you love" and "find beauty in everything" were becoming distant echoes in Mia's mind. And her path was leading her straight to a future that alarmingly mirrored the unhappy, wearisome lives her parents had lived.

Then again, it wasn't as if having a steady job and good

friends was any great hardship. Especially when compared to Gavin's life.

Her heart squeezed tight, like a fist.

"Hello? Earth to Mia." Danny waved his hand in front of her face.

"Oh, sorry." Mia blinked and shook her head. "Just thinking of something else."

Danny's mouth twisted wryly. "Good to know I'm such fabulous company."

"I'm sorry. The wedding has just taken over my life these days."

"Hey, you need a date for the main event?" Danny's ears turned pink. "I mean, not a real date, just like a *plus one* or whatever it's called. Not that I don't want to go on a real date with you because who wouldn't? But no pressure. Just offering if you need someone to go along to the wedding and dance the maid-of-honor dance with you or whatever...okay, I'll shut up now."

Mia smiled, unable to help being charmed by his bumbling. "Thanks, but I'm going solo. I just want to be there for Polly and make sure everything runs smoothly. It's nothing personal."

"Yeah, sure." He downed the last of his beer, his ears still pink. "Maybe we could go out to dinner instead sometime?"

Two days ago, she would have said yes. At the very least she would have agreed to meet him for drinks again. Now...

"Thank you," she said. "But actually...wedding aside, I'm seeing someone."

"Oh." His face fell. "I should've figured, huh?"

"Sorry we're late!"

Mia looked up in relief as Susan and Anna sailed toward the table, their gazes going from Mia to Danny.

"Look at you, girl, already with the company," Anna remarked.

"Danny was just leaving," Mia said in an effort to avoid further awkwardness.

He gave them all a sheepish grin and stood, giving Mia a little tip of his head. "If you change your mind…"

He saluted her with his beer and returned to the bar.

"Hottie!" Susan sat down, slinging her purse over the back of the chair. "Did you give him your number?"

Mia shook her head. Her friends ordered drinks, chattered about their day, complained about their bosses, discussed weekend plans. Normally Mia would have been right in the middle of the socializing, but all she could think about was the clock inching toward nine o'clock.

Finally with apologies, she left the bar and walked back to her car. Darkness had fallen and most of the shops had closed. Pedestrians continued to stroll along Ocean Avenue, going in and out of restaurants and cafés.

Mia turned off the main street toward the lot where she'd parked her car. Full during the workday, now only three other vehicles sat in the lot.

She took her keys from her purse and quickened her pace.

"Hey, Mia!"

Alarm shot through her as the male voice echoed through the parking lot. She turned.

Danny was jogging toward her, his hand up. Though relieved it was only him, instinct had Mia moving more rapidly toward her car.

"You forgot your cell phone," he called.

Her hand went automatically to her bag. She didn't remember taking her phone out at the bar.

"I overheard your friends, and I told them I'd bring it out to you." Danny came to a stop a short distance away. "Sorry, didn't mean to freak you out."

Mia's unease deepened. Though she and Danny were acquaintances, she didn't know him *that* well. Certainly not well enough to feel comfortable alone with him in a deserted parking lot. She slipped her hand into her purse. Her fingers touched her cell phone.

What the...?

Her heart jolted into her throat. She fumbled to find the right key to insert into the car door.

"Why'd you leave so soon?" he asked.

"I need to go."

"Look, I'm sorry if I came on too strong back there." He moved toward her, his hands still up like he was surrendering. "It's just that I've seen you around so much, and I've been working up the courage to ask you out. But I don't have your number, and there's no guarantee I'll see you again. So even if you break up with your boyfriend, I wouldn't have a chance if I can't contact you. And I really want a chance."

"Danny, there's no chance," Mia snapped. "Stay away from me."

His expression darkened, his skin pallid and yellowish in the glow of the overhead lights.

Mia pushed the key into the lock, relieved when it turned. She quickly got into the car, slamming and locking the door behind her. Danny was right outside the door now, still saying something. As if she'd listen.

Hands shaking, Mia started the engine and sped out of the parking lot. Her skin prickled with apprehension. She could still feel him watching her.

CHAPTER 10

$\mathcal{M}$ ia stopped at a red light, her heart hammering. She grabbed her phone out of her bag and called Anna.

"What?" her friend yelled. "Sorry, I can't hear you. It's really loud in here."

"That guy Danny," Mia said. "Did he say anything to you?"

"I wish," Anna shouted. "I think he left right after you did. Why? Did you see him again?"

"No, but if he comes back to the bar, avoid him. He's creepy."

"Oh no. What happened? Are you okay?"

"I'm fine. Just warning you that I have a bad feeling about him. Stay safe."

Mia ended the call, not wanting to upset her friends with details about the encounter. She drove home and hurried into her apartment, her heart rate calming only when she was back inside her familiar surroundings.

She undressed and took a hot shower, tilting her head up to the spray and letting the water wash away the unpleasantness of her day. She dressed in pink and black checkered flannel pants and a soft pink fleece decorated with little cupcakes.

When the knock came at her door, happiness lit inside her. She opened the door and stepped aside, letting her gaze roam hungrily over Gavin in his black shirt and trousers that fit his muscular body to perfection.

"Hi." Her voice was breathless.

His gaze slipped over her appreciatively before he pressed a hard, possessive kiss against her lips. Pleasure zinged through her.

"How was work?" She closed the door behind him.

"We have a problem." He set his steel briefcase on a table and turned to face her, his expression tightening behind his glasses.

Mia's heart plummeted. "What kind of problem?"

He studied her, a crease appearing between his eyebrows. "What happened?"

"What?"

"Something upset you. I want to know what it is."

Mia blinked. "Seriously? Are you psychic?"

He smiled faintly. "No. But I can sense when you're troubled. And I hope you trust me enough to tell me why."

She stared at the Knight Security logo on his shirt, remembering the past that had led him to form his own protective services company. This hardened soldier had built a career of keeping people safe. It couldn't have been a more perfect fit.

She wanted desperately to sink into his arms and let him take her bad day away, but suddenly it seemed silly compared to everything he was dealing with. She was an adult who could handle a little unpleasantness by herself.

"It's nothing." She waved a hand, forcing a light note into her voice. "So what's this problem you have now?"

He studied her for a moment, clearly not believing her dismissal, before turning to open his briefcase.

"I don't like all the new changes to the layout, especially at this stage," he said. "We need to get rid of several things that will pose a security hazard."

Her stomach dropped. "Are you kidding me right now?"

"Last I understood, there were three hundred guests, with eight people per table. This plan accounts for three hundred fifty people and has a row of tables lined up near the windows."

"You can blame Julia Bennett for that," Mia said. "She wanted to add people to the guest list, and of course Polly accommodated her."

"And why did you open up the adjoining room, which has access to the outside?"

"To create more space, of course. The reception will be in the main hall and foyer, with the doors open to the gardens and courtyard."

"I was told the courtyard would be closed after the ceremony."

"That was the old plan." She crossed her arms, steeling her spine with determination. "Now we need the courtyard for the cocktail hour. There are about a dozen people I'm trying to keep happy here, and if that means opening up the outside, then that's what we have to do. Why can't you just reassign your team or whatever?"

His jaw tightened. "Security planning has to be done well in advance to ensure we have all the resources and lines of communication intact. Any break in the chain of command creates a loophole that I won't tolerate. We need to rearrange the reception layout. I want that row of ceramic planters removed from the courtyard, and I want those tables moved into the foyer. We need to expand the pathways into the garden and create a barrier at the edge of the field. Also, no fireworks."

Disappointment crashed down on her. Her eyes stung.

"The...the fireworks are a surprise."

"I don't like surprises."

"They're not for *you*," Mia retorted. "They're for Polly and Luke. For the whole party. They'll be way out on the ocean, nowhere near the party itself."

"Why isn't the information on the spreadsheet?" Gavin asked. "I just heard about it from Evan Stone."

"I didn't want to put it with the other wedding plans in case Polly saw it."

"So why didn't you tell me?"

"I'm sorry, I forgot."

"You forgot to tell me about *fireworks*?"

The disbelieving note in his voice made her insides shrivel up. Of course Mr. Stoic Regimented Commander would never forget anything.

"I'm not in charge of it." She searched her bookshelf for the folder containing the fireworks information. "An old friend of Luke's contacted Hannah a couple of weeks ago, asking if he could provide the fireworks show as a wedding present. We thought it was a great idea, and Hannah has been scrambling to get all the permits to make it happen. With all the other planning, I left that up to her."

"I need to know *everything*." Gavin took off his glasses and pinched the bridge of his nose. "The guy Brian Hurst showed up at Sugar Rush the other day to see Evan, but Evan didn't know why until he'd talked to Hannah. So if I allowed Hurst to do his fireworks show, I'd have to run checks on him and everyone else involved."

"But the fireworks will be nowhere near the villa."

"Doesn't matter. My job is to ensure the complete security of this event."

"My job is to ensure my best friend has a perfect wedding."

"Moving planters and tables will have no impact on the perfection of the wedding itself. And since Luke and Polly don't even know about the fireworks yet, they won't miss anything."

Mia's frustration exploded. She turned, throwing the folder at him in a fit of pique. It hit his chest and fell to the floor. His eyes narrowed.

"*What* is your problem?" she snapped. "Look, I understand

that security is important, and God knows I don't want anything
to happen to anyone but you're treating this wedding like it's the
freaking Pentagon. Why? What's happened between a year ago
and now that suddenly has you sending in armored tanks?"

Her heart pounded, her vision blurring. A muscle ticked in
Gavin's jaw, but otherwise he showed no emotion. Tension thickened the air.

Unable to bear his silence, Mia spun on her heel and went
into her bedroom, slamming and locking the door behind her.
She sank onto the bed and blinked back hot tears.

The doorknob rattled. "Mia, open the door."

"No." She crossed her arms mutinously, not caring if she was
being *petulant*. Or having a full-out tantrum. "Go away."

The knob rattled again, then there was a scraping noise and a
click. The door swung open. Gavin stood there like a shadow, his
expression set in a frown.

She turned away from him. He approached, stopping in front
of her. In his black shirt and trousers, he was a dark storm cloud
against the paisley purple wallpaper and canopied bed.

He put his hand under her chin, forcing her to look up at him.

"Never lock me out," he said.

She swallowed, struck by the gravity in his eyes, the sense that
he wasn't only talking about her bedroom door.

"I don't want you here anymore," she muttered.

"Too bad."

He continued looking at her, as if he didn't need to do
anything else to make her yield.

As it turned out, he didn't.

"Fine," she said, her throat tight. "I'll move the tables and
planters. But you're going to have to tell Luke's friend and
Hannah about the fireworks."

His hand was warm and big under her chin, like a cradle.

"Tell me what else is going on," he said.

It wasn't a question. Her earlier resistance weakened. Strange how he made everything, no matter how gentle, into a command. Even stranger how that softened her inside, made her want to be malleable and pliant.

"It's just been lousy day," she confessed, a sob catching in her throat. "I misfiled something at work that was due, so it didn't go out on time and one of the accountants chewed me out. Then Polly was off doing something with Luke, and I haven't done anything with her in weeks...and I spent all this time thinking about things I'm good at, and when I sent the list to you, you didn't respond.

"I ripped a hole in my favorite scarf, and now there's all this stuff you want to change about the wedding...and it's just so *stupid* of me to complain about things like that when I can't even imagine how awful things were for you, and whatever is going on with the wedding has to be bad or you wouldn't be such a hardass, and here I am whining that my best friend is going out with her fiancé and I got yelled at in a job I hate anyway, but last night was so freaking amazing and today was such crap that I—"

Her voice broke. Gavin grasped her shoulders and pulled her to her feet. She stared at the hollow of his throat. A pulse beat rapidly there; the only evidence of his emotions. By contrast, she was a hot mess—her breath hitched, tears stung her eyes, and she was trembling with impotent distress.

Then he tugged her closer, so swiftly that she fell against him. The instant her body made contact with his solid strength, her misery faded, as if he were absorbing it into himself, taking it from her. He embraced her, his arms like steel and velvet, locking her against him.

"You're allowed to be upset by a bad day." He rubbed his cheek against her hair. "Should you feel guilty for being upset? No. Can it help to compare your situation to others? Yes. Do you need to? No. You never have to apologize for the way you feel."

Her tears overflowed, but this time from relief rather than

angst. She pressed her face to the front of his shirt and drew in a shuddering breath.

"How'd you get to be so smart?" she mumbled.

"Who says I'm smart?"

"I do." She slipped her arms around his waist and hugged him tightly. "And you are."

He rubbed his big hand up and down her back. "Then tell me what else happened."

She would never have secrets from him. She didn't want to. After all those months of trying to get his attention, she now had his attention right to the center of her soul. She only hoped she could keep it.

"I…I had an unpleasant encounter," she admitted.

He stiffened, pulling back slightly to look at her. "Tell me."

"After work, I went to meet some friends for happy hour." Mia shivered, tightening her arms around him. "This creepy guy followed me to the parking lot."

Everything about Gavin changed in an instant. Steel infused his expression, his body tensing and eyes icing over.

"What did he do?" His voice remained calm and steady.

"He just spooked me. Said he wanted to return my cell phone, but he didn't have it. I left as fast as I could."

"What bar?"

"Asante, on First Street. I go there all the time."

"What was his name?"

"Danny. I don't know his last name. I've seen him around before, but that was the first time he'd come after me."

Gavin was silent for a moment, as if he were processing that information like a computer. Then he pulled away from her.

"Stay here," he ordered. "Lock the door behind me, and don't open it for anyone."

"Where are you…"

He walked swiftly out of the bedroom. The front door closed.

"…going?" Mia finished to the empty room.

She gave a choked laugh and shook her head, wiping her eyes with her sleeve. Because she had some instinctive need to obey him, she locked the front door. Her temporary sense of calm dissipated, fresh unease prickling her skin. So much for anticipating a nice evening alone with him.

His briefcase still sat on the coffee table, which surely meant he was coming back. She paced back and forth, then tried to kill some time by watching *The Princess Bride*.

Finally, after an hour had passed, a knock came at the door. She hurried to open it.

Gavin entered, carrying two paper grocery bags, and crossed to the kitchen.

Mia followed him. "Where did you go?"

"Asante, to see if I could track down that little fucker Danny." He set the bags on the counter. "Unfortunately he wasn't there and no one recalled seeing him. I'll hunt around more tomorrow."

"What…what would you do if you found him?"

"Teach him a lesson." His hard tone indicated it would be one hell of a lesson. He turned to face her, his expression stern. "From now on, you don't walk to your car unless you're with a friend. If you're alone, you call me and wait in a safe place until I get there. Understand?"

She pressed her lips together. "I know how to handle myself when I go out."

"Do you understand?" His eyes narrowed into slits of cobalt.

"Yes, I understand." She put her chin up, a hint of belligerence rising inside her. "But don't think you get to fuck me one time and then start telling me what to do *all* the time."

"Make no mistake, sweetheart." Gavin brushed a lock of hair away from her face, his tone shifting to one of measured certainty. "This is more than a one-time fuck. And there will be times when I tell you what to do. Keyword—*tell*. I'm not asking. I don't tolerate dissent, especially not when your safety is at risk.

You can fight me all you want, but nothing you do will change the fact that I will protect you to the fullest extent of my abilities. If that means making you angry with me, then fine. I can take it."

She had no doubt about that. Gavin could take anything and everything and still remain as steady as a boulder. It was just one of the qualities that drew her to him like a magnet—underlying her fear of a life opposite the one she wanted lay the vague sense of being adrift. Being with Gavin was like holding on to an immovable anchor.

He brushed his knuckles across her cheek and turned to open the grocery bags.

"What's all that?" she asked.

"Good food." He opened her refrigerator and started transferring food from the bags—eggs, milk, organic chicken, yogurt, carrots, broccoli. He placed other items on the counter and in the cupboards—apples and bananas, granola, nuts, wheat crackers.

"You went grocery shopping for me?"

"Apparently you can't be bothered to do it yourself," he replied dryly, folding the bags. "Have you eaten dinner yet?"

"I had a calamari plate at Asante," Mia said.

"And?"

"A lemon drop martini."

Disapproval creased his brow. "You need to take better care of yourself."

He was right, much as she didn't love being reminded of that. It was clear he took exceptional care of himself both through clean eating and regular workouts that gave him that incredible, rock-solid physique. But those habits appeared borne of his past trauma—a way to control his life since there had once been a time when he'd had little, if any, control at all.

Maybe that was also why he was so authoritative and demanding—she'd seen his controlling nature in his interactions with his men, and she was now starting to experience it herself. The realization made her both uneasy and terribly excited.

"Sit down." He motioned to the table before uncorking a bottle of wine. "I'll make dinner."

She sat, accepting the glass of wine he put in front of her. He took ingredients out of the fridge and started chopping and slicing.

"*The Princess Bride?*" he asked, nodding to the archway through which the TV was visible.

"You've really never seen it?"

"Maybe. Can't remember."

Mia made a huffing noise of annoyance. "If you'd seen it, you'd remember. It's an epic, swashbuckling tale of true love."

Skepticism flashed over his face. "Is that the one with the big rats in a forest?"

"Rodents of Unusual Size." She glowered at him. "Are you kidding me? You *have* seen it and you don't remember?"

"It's been a while." He tossed slices of zucchini into a hot pan. "Epic, swashbuckling tales of true love aren't my thing."

She tried not to take *that* remark too much to heart. Apparently not realizing the implications of what he'd just said, Gavin continued cooking and soon had a dinner of baked chicken, roasted zucchini, and rice on the table.

Mia pushed aside her unease so she could enjoy Gavin taking care of her again. Even though her apartment was her domain, her haven from the world, she really liked him there. She liked him cooking in her kitchen and sitting at the table. She liked watching him eat, his movements sharp and methodical, her decorative floral silverware held securely in his big hands.

It was kind of a turn on, too—watching the spoon slide between his lips, his jaw muscles shifting as he chewed, the pressure of his fingers on the knife. And at times like this, she liked his silence, the compatibility of just sitting and eating dinner together.

She pushed her empty plate away with a sigh of pleasure. "That was delicious. I feel much better."

"Good." He rose to take their plates to the sink. "Because we still need to talk about the wedding."

Mia groaned. She crossed her arms on the table and lowered her head onto them. "You know, planning the wedding *used* to be fun."

"I want to give you whatever you want," Gavin rested his hand on her hair, stroking it away from her face. "I know you have a vision for this wedding, that you want it to be beautiful and remarkable and all those good things. I love that you see the world that way. I never want to take that away from you. But the reality of my job is to protect against threats."

Mia heard every word he said, but two stood out like flashing neon signs. *I love.* Never once had she imagined Gavin Knight saying he *loved* anything. Heck, she'd spent months wondering if there was anything in the world he even *liked a little bit.* And now he'd just said he *loved* her view of the world.

Her heart was beating fast, and not only because he was stroking her hair with such easy tenderness. She kept her face in the crook of her arm, absorbing his touch, before slowly turning to look at him.

"Tell me," she whispered. "Trust me enough to tell me."

He ran his hand over her cheek, a troubled gleam appearing in his eyes.

"The owners of Sugar Rush occasionally get angry letters or emails," he finally said. "Sometimes from people who think someone in the company has wronged them. Most of the time, they're just looking to extort money."

"What about the other times?"

"Every now and then, someone really believes they've been wronged," Gavin explained. "That appears to be the case now. A man is claiming Luke stole his idea for something called Zigzag Candy. Of course, Luke has never stolen anything from anyone, much less a candy idea. And though the company has a ton of evidence to support that, the guy's not buying it. He's sent a few letters and emails about it over the months, but with the wedding getting closer, his attempts to incite a response have escalated."

"To the level of a risk?"

"To the level that we need to take extra security precautions."

A chill prickled down Mia's spine. She sensed the undercurrent of his words, that this "threat" was far more dangerous than he'd initially led her to believe.

"So why...why didn't you tell me that at the beginning?" she asked.

"The details are locked down," Gavin said. "Polly doesn't even know the threat level at this point, and I intend to keep it that way. It may seem otherwise, but you and I have the same goal. We both want Polly and Luke to have a perfect wedding."

She considered that, liking the notion that they were on the same side. That they'd been on the same side this whole time. "So what do we do now?"

"I will try my damnedest to give you what you want." He curled a lock of her hair around his finger and tugged. "But you need to understand that you have to compromise. If you don't, I'll have to get medieval on your pretty ass."

"Hmm." She arched an eyebrow. "Sounds promising."

"In that case," he murmured, lowering his head to press a warm kiss to her lips, "I might just do it anyway."

CHAPTER 11

"If you take out the planters and topiary, you can string the lights along this row of trees and around the windows." Gavin pointed to the map denoting the exterior of the villa. "I'm okay with you keeping the courtyard open, but I'll be stationing three extra men at the perimeter. The entire interior team is composed of fully trained close protection operatives. They will also all be dressed appropriately and look like regular guests."

Mia leaned forward on the sofa to study the map that was spread out on the coffee table. She'd gotten out all the wedding binders, and they'd been reviewing the entire event from start to finish.

"What about the entry from the parking lot?"

He explained the revised plans for access control, and though Mia didn't love the idea of checkpoints, she understood the need for them.

It also looked as if everything would be okay if she didn't fight Gavin on every change and they worked together instead. She conceded that it must be a pain for him to have to modify all the security measures because of last-minute changes to the plan.

And of course she didn't want anything even slightly bad to happen at the wedding.

She gave him new contact information for several of the vendors, confirmed that only certain people would be making deliveries, and agreed to his changes in access control.

"Where will you be during the event?" She gestured to the map.

"I have a command center set up here." He tapped a room beside the kitchen. "But I'll be patrolling the whole area and in communication with all teams."

"And the fireworks?" Mia asked.

"I'll review the details and talk to both Hannah and the guy who's organizing them," Gavin said. "I won't make promises, but if it checks out okay, you can still have the fireworks."

She smiled, the last threads of tension easing from her chest. "Even though they're a surprise?"

"As you said, they're not for me." He rolled up the map and set it back in his briefcase. "I can handle surprises for other people, as long as no one's safety is compromised."

"I'm glad you're the one in charge." Mia liked his efficient movements, his large, capable hands that could perform any task. She pulled her knees up to her chest and wrapped her arms around them, feeling tired but satisfied at what they had accomplished. "I know everything will be fine in your hands."

He shot her an amused grin. "You didn't think that at first."

"Yes, I did. I didn't like you messing with my plans, but I've always known you can handle anything, especially protecting other people. There's nothing you can't do. It's just one of the reasons I've liked you for so long."

He closed his briefcase and turned to slide his hands around her ankles. He tugged her feet onto his lap.

"Trust me, sweetheart." He rested his head on the back of the sofa. "There are a thousand things I can't do."

"Well, making me feel good, both physically and emotionally, isn't one of them. Because you do that *so* well."

A faint, humorless smile tugged at his mouth. He stroked his hands over her bare feet, trailing his fingers along the curves of her ankles and arches.

"What am I going to do with you?" he murmured under his breath, slipping his hand beneath the hem of her fleece pajama pants.

"Whatever you want."

He let out a short laugh. "You got under my skin the second I saw you sitting on the counter at the bakery, batting your eyelashes at me."

Mia smiled at the memory, remembering the zing of excitement she'd felt when she first saw Gavin, all steely-eyed and muscular, stride into Wild Child with his security team.

"When you started talking about the bakery security system, you said you had to conduct a *physical assessment*," she said. "And I told you that sounded fun."

"Mmm. I stripped you naked in my head right then and there. Gave you my own personal physical assessment."

"I wouldn't have known that by looking at you." Mia nudged her toes against his groin. "Given that you merely asked me if I was an employee, then told Polly you were going to check staffing security levels. I think that was the instant I decided to do whatever I could to get your attention."

"Honey, you had my attention with one look. If only you knew what I've imagined doing to you…"

"You don't have to imagine them anymore." Mia wiggled her foot, a tingle racing up her leg as his cock swelled under the light pressure. "You can just do them."

He rubbed his fingers over the soles of her feet in a warm, gentle massage.

"Your list," he said.

"Which one?" Mia settled back against the sofa pillow. "The guest list?"

"No, the one you texted me at noon."

"Oh. I didn't even know you got it."

"I did." He glanced at her, still rubbing her feet. "So how did it feel to write those things?"

That was what he wanted to talk about now?

"Well…okay, I guess. I mean, I had to think pretty hard, which wasn't all that fun."

"And how do you feel about what you came up with?"

"Fine. It's all true. I'm good at all those things." She rolled the hem of her fleece between her fingers. "So why didn't you respond?"

He studied her with that *seeing into her soul* gaze that stirred a new longing inside her. A longing to let him into all the places where her fears and insecurities lurked, the ones she usually kept concealed beneath a candy-colored veneer of fun and pleasure.

"I wanted you to think about them," Gavin said. "You're using all those qualities right now."

"What are you even talking about?"

"By planning the wedding. You're an excellent organizer, good with people and decorating. You also know how to manage your time. You're a great friend who knows how to make this about Polly, not you. And yes, you make the bad stuff disappear, which is what people want when they're planning a special event."

"So what does that have to do with anything?"

"It proves you don't have to blame yourself for deciding to major in French lit and not developing work experience. You have a skill set. Now you need to put it to more permanent use."

"I don't know how."

"Think about it."

"Are you trying to psychoanalyze me again?"

"Your beautiful brain doesn't need psychoanalysis. You just need to know what you want. And to know you can do it."

She looked at the ceiling as she considered what he'd said.

Maybe he was right that she was using all those qualities with the wedding—more, she'd genuinely enjoyed doing it, not only for her best friend's sake but for her own. She'd loved processing all of Polly's ideas, then working with decorators, florists, caterers, and musicians to fulfill her friend's vision of a perfect wedding. She couldn't have been more thorough with the details and dedicated to ensuring the event unfolded without a hitch.

"When Granny turned seventy-five, I planned a surprise birthday party for her," she told Gavin. "She loved wild animals, so the party was zoo-themed. It was so much fun. We had a zebra cake and I put all this greenery by the door so it was like the guests were entering a jungle. We had animal games and party favors. Everyone loved it. So I'm good at this kind of stuff. Planning events and parties."

"You are."

"Do you think I could do it for a living?" Excitement sparked inside her, and she sat up to look at him. "I mean, as a career?"

"Do you think you could?" Gavin asked.

"I could try," Mia said. "Maybe see if there are any event planners looking to hire an assistant. Or maybe just do it myself. If I could put Luke and Polly's wedding on my resume, that's already an amazing reference. My friend Susan's parents have a 40th anniversary coming up. I can ask her if she needs help with the planning." She chewed on her bottom lip, considering. "What do you think?"

"I think it's a great idea."

"I'm not even sure where to start."

"Sounds like you already have," Gavin said.

She had, hadn't she? She wasn't well-versed about starting her own business, but Polly was now a highly successful businesswoman and could give her plenty of advice. And all their other friends would be happy to help out. She'd always liked going out and having fun with their friends, but she knew they'd rally around her if she needed them.

She rubbed her hands on her pants. "I've never thought of starting my own business before. I know from Polly that it's a ton of work, but I'm a good worker. Especially when I'm working for something I believe in. I think I can do it."

"I know you can."

She looked at him, struck by the satisfaction in his blue eyes, the relaxed set of his shoulders.

"Did you have that idea all along?" she asked.

"I figured you could do something like that, yes. But the idea had to be yours."

"I think you lied. You really are psychic."

He smiled. "I'd never lie to you."

He certainly hadn't yet. In fact, he'd been nothing but honest, sometimes painfully so. She got to her knees and moved across the sofa to him. He opened his arms. She settled against him, her curves fitting perfectly against the hard planes of his chest. Warmth flooded her, banishing any lingering frustration.

"Thank you," she said.

He kissed the top of her head and folded his arms around her. And just like that, all the bad stuff disappeared.

CHAPTER 12

*D*uring the day, Gavin had a laser-sharp focus on finalizing the security for Luke and Polly's wedding. Nothing, not even Mia Donovan in pink fleece cupcake pajamas, could distract him when he was working.

Then there was a point when he stopped working. And she flooded his thoughts like a waterfall breaking through a cliff.

On Saturday, he paid another visit to Asante and a few other downtown bars, interrogating the bartenders and servers about a kid who fit "Danny's" description, but came up empty.

A search through his online resources revealed dozens of "Dannys" and "Daniels" in the area. Though he had no official reason to have the kid arrested, he wasn't above issuing a warning and scaring him.

He set one of his men to further searching before he left the Knight Security offices. Unless he was coordinating his team at a venue or event, he was accustomed to working until seven or eight, even on weekends, then heading home to cook dinner before trying to wind down with a hot shower or TV. Invariably he ended up working most of the night, in between sporadic sleep.

He closed the front door and set his keys and briefcase down. His phone buzzed with a text from Luke—*Don't forget BBQ tomorrow at Dad's. 5pm.*

Gavin texted back: *Thanks, but working late.*

He could almost hear the exasperation in Luke's tone with the reply: *Tomorrow is Saturday.*

He punched out another text. *And the wedding is in a week.*

No reply came after that. Not even Luke could argue with the timeline of his own wedding.

Gavin told himself his distance from the Stones was due to professional reasons; he'd spent the past five years setting up his business and reworking the entire Sugar Rush security system. Didn't matter that it was finished now—maintaining security and keeping all protocols up to date was a major part of his job.

He unknotted his tie, poured a glass of scotch, and checked his mail and messages. There was another thick envelope with his name scrawled in black ink. He opened it and dumped out the contents.

His blood iced. Photos of wedding preparations spilled onto the counter—the decorator leaving her shop, the villa manager, two women sitting at a table at Wild Child. Polly and...Mia.

Anger bubbled inside him. How the fuck...?

He opened the single sheet of paper. The black ink read:

Are you ready? Because I am.

Gavin smothered his anger. He set the note and photographs aside. He had to stay dispassionate. Letting his personal feelings take over could only lead to mistakes.

He'd promised Polly her wedding would be perfect. And he'd vowed to protect Mia to the fullest extent of his abilities. He'd keep his promises, even if it meant shutting off everything he was starting to feel for her.

He'd be an idiot to underestimate his adversary. This could be a diversion—that another area could be a target while the wedding was in progress. He already had a stronger security presence and police at Sugar Rush and the Stones' private residences, both now and on the day of the event.

He took a hot shower, changed into pajama bottoms and a T-shirt, and sat down to both finish his scotch and review the rest of the security measures. He logged in to the map of the Sugar Rush campus. The doorbell rang.

His guard shot up. He peered through the peephole and yanked the door open.

"What are you doing here?" he snapped.

Mia blinked her green eyes at him. "Hello to you too."

"It's almost eleven."

"I know. You showed up on my doorstep at *almost eleven*, remember?" She pushed past him in a waft of cheese and pepperoni, her arms laden with a large pizza box and a paper bag. "I decided it was about time I brought dinner to you. Pizza and a special treat from this little hole-in-the-wall bakery up in Santa Cruz. They just made fresh batch about an hour ago."

He frowned. "You drove all the way up to Santa Cruz alone just to get dessert?"

"See how much I like you?" She gave him a sweet smile. He hardened his heart against its potent effect.

"I don't like you driving alone so late." He closed the door and followed her into the kitchen. "Much less going forty miles away to some hole-in-the-wall."

"I have my cell, Gavin." She narrowed her eyes and took two plates from the cupboard. "And it's not like you cared last week what I did or didn't do alone. Or at what time."

"That was before we were..." *Shit. What?*

Mia lifted an eyebrow. "Before we were what?"

"Before we were a *thing*," he retorted.

"Oh my." She pressed a hand to her heart, her eyes widening. "Are we really a *thing*, Mr. Knight? Why, I just might swoon."

He crossed his arms and scowled. "You know what I mean."

"Yes, my Roman emperor." She put her hand on his arm, stood on tiptoe, and kissed his nose. "I know what you mean."

She bustled around the kitchen, getting out napkins and glasses, taking romaine lettuce from the fridge to make a salad. In a red mini-dress, sheer stockings, and red flats, she was a valentine come to life. One who was starting to fold into his heart at the worst possible time.

He tilted his head back and swallowed the last of his scotch. He shouldn't have crossed the line. He'd known that even when he was stepping over it.

And that wasn't how he operated. Ever. So why was he taking risks for this little flowers-and-lace girl? Yeah, she fucked like a dream, but he could get some action anywhere. Instead he'd let his dick rule his head, and now he'd likely put her at a level of danger that made his blood freeze.

"Sit down before it gets cold." Mia waved him to the table.

She poured herself a glass of wine from the bottle he'd left on the counter the other night and sat across from him.

Tell her to go.

The order snapped into his head, but his voice refused to issue the words. All he could do was try to smother the pleasure at the realization that he only needed to look up to see her sitting across from him.

What if it could always be like that? What if she snuggled up against him every night and he woke to the all-encompassing scent and feel of her? What if she walked sleepy-eyed into the kitchen every morning, pressing a soft kiss against his jaw before asking for coffee? What if she texted him little notes throughout the day, asked him to join her for lunch, gave him little glances that only they understood? What if he could take care of her forev—

Christ. He was turning into a sappy, lovesick asshole. One

who had no idea how he was going to extricate himself from this young woman who'd made his heart beat again.

"I had my final fitting for my dress this afternoon." Mia lifted a slice of pizza to her mouth, oblivious of his inner commotion. "And I confirmed all the changes with Polly, who is fine with everything. She's scheduled the rehearsal dinner for two nights before so we all get enough sleep before the main event. She's all excited because Luke is surprising her with the honeymoon, so she has no idea where they're going. If I had to guess, it's probably Spain because I overheard him talking to Hannah about Barcelona."

Gavin was accustomed to dead silence when he came home from work, but Mia's chatter was like music. At Wild Child, he'd always enjoyed the sound of her voice and her silvery laugh. He didn't dare imagine what it would be like to have the *sound of her* filling his house all the time.

"So what did you do today?" she asked.

"Worked."

She nibbled on a pizza crust. "Do you ever do anything besides work?"

"Not really. Though that's changed somewhat over the past few days."

Her eyebrows drew together slightly. "But before we were a thing. Don't you have any hobbies?"

"I work out at the gym. Used to do a lot of running, but on my last tour I blew out my knees."

"Is that why you were medically discharged?"

He nodded.

She glanced at her plate, fidgeting with the edge of her napkin. "Can I ask you what happened?"

His jaw tightened. He didn't want anything staining her beauty, but this was his reality. It always would be. At some point, she needed to know the truth.

"A nasty surprise." He pushed back the black fog encroaching on his mind. "We were on a recon mission in a town outside of Fallujah. We'd pulled up near an abandoned building for the night. I was on the roof when the mortar blast hit. The building crumbled like a house of cards. The floor went out from under me. Broke both legs, shattered my knees. I was sent back for replacement surgery."

"And the PTSD?"

"Yeah." He dragged a hand down his face. "That was from everything else."

Shit. He hated the despair in her green eyes, the lines of sorrow on her forehead. He no longer wanted to keep her in a tower—he wanted her out in the world, charming people with her smile and helping them celebrate their lives. She belonged in a dream land, a place with cotton-candy clouds and an endless supply of ice cream. Not his world. Not a world where she was a potential target for a psychopath.

A psychopath who knew Gavin's fucking home address.

He shoved off the stool and took his plate to the sink. "Come on. I'll drive you home."

She blinked. "I don't want to go home."

"Too bad." He picked up his keys from the counter.

Mia frowned, a mutinous glint appearing in her eyes. "I came to spend the night."

"You're not spending the night."

"Why not?"

"Because I need to be at work early tomorrow."

"So I'll make you chocolate-chip pancakes before you leave."

Goddammit.

He could see it. Mia in his kitchen, wearing one of his T-shirts, her hair loose and tangled down her back, that little furrow between her eyes as she studied the frying pancakes and lifted a corner of one to see if it was ready to flip. Turning to smile at him when he walked in, lifting her face for his kiss, her eyes bright and happy. His sunrise.

His bones almost cracked with the desperate force of *wanting* that scenario more than he wanted to breathe.

He tightened his fist on his keys. "You're going home."

"I am not." She crossed her arms and glared.

"Do I need to pick you up and carry you out to my car?" he snapped.

"No, you big bully, because I'm not leaving."

He dropped the keys and moved toward her so fast he didn't have time to think. Mia gave a little shriek and jumped off her stool, racing around to the other side of the central island to put it between them. She lifted her brows in challenge, color rising to her cheeks.

"Ha." The word escaped her on a breath. "All the times you ignored me when I would have leapt right into whatever net you held out. Now you can't catch me, can you, Mr. Knight?"

Gavin stopped and gripped the edge of the granite counter. "I'm not playing with you, Mia."

"You're not?" Her eyes widened in mock innocence. "You mean all this fucking and flirting we've been doing is *serious*?"

She was killing him. Wresting control from him. *Weakening* him.

"Get your pretty ass into the car," he ordered.

"Make me."

"I don't have time for games." He flexed and unflexed his fingers on the counter's edge.

"Then you shouldn't have started one." She tossed her golden hair and stuck her tongue out at him.

"Brat." He started around the central island toward her.

Mia gasped, her eyes glittering with excitement as they circled the island like a cat and mouse. She darted away from him every time he moved, her escapes punctuated by little laughs of triumph.

Though he wasn't exerting himself physically, Gavin's breath increased. He stopped again, his jaw clenching. A twisted combination of anger and lust brewed inside him.

"Enough," he said. "You either get in the car or you sleep on the sofa. Your choice."

"I came here to sleep with *you*." Mia pursed her lips into a pout. "Why are you fighting the chance to sink your big cock into my tight wet pussy?"

"That is *it*, little girl." Gavin rushed around the counter, grabbing her by the waist before she could escape.

He hauled her back against his chest. Mia shrieked, trying to pull away. She was no match for his size and strength, but she struggled like a hellion, clawing at his arms and kicking her legs. Gavin ignored both the writhing of her body and his own lust-fueled reaction. He tightened his hold, lifting her off the floor and striding toward the living room.

"Let me go, you jerk." Panting, Mia wiggled and twisted in his grip. "I came here with pizza and romantic intentions, and you have the nerve to snap at me and order me to get in the fucking car. Why are you being so mean?"

"I'm not being *mean*," he replied evenly. "I don't like that you came here alone so late at night. I also don't like that you're refusing to listen."

He couldn't tell her about the goddamned letter and photos that intensified his fear a hundredfold. If anything happened to anyone under his watch, he'd never be able to live with the guilt.

But if anything happened to *Mia*, he'd lose his fucking mind.

He sank onto the sofa, his arms still wrapped around her from behind, and waited for her to calm down. But his girl was revved up to fight, her body tense with frustration and her breathing hard.

"Let me go," she snapped, straining against the circle of his arms.

"Stop fighting."

"No!" She dug her fingernails into his arm, hard enough to sting.

Gavin's spine tensed. He wrestled her around and took hold of her chin, forcing her to look at him. Her green eyes blazed with rage and hurt.

"Stop," he commanded.

"Fuck you."

Steel infused his veins. "You just made a big mistake."

"Yeah, hooking up with a control freak security asshole who thinks he can order people around like army soldiers."

"Marines," he corrected.

"What*ever*. Let me go!"

She wiggled on his lap, a movement that made her skirt ride up on her thighs. His dick reacted predictably, though his brain was more focused on both teaching her that he didn't tolerate disrespect and showing her what kind of man he really was. Then she'd run away from him as fast as she could.

He maneuvered her around so she was lying facedown across his lap, his growing erection pushing against her soft belly.

"What are you..." Mia gasped, bucking her hips upward.

He clamped one arm around her waist to hold her in place and gathered her skirt in his other fist. She struggled, bracing her hands on the floor, her long hair falling forward to veil her face.

"Don't move," he ordered, pinching her thigh.

"You're not going to..." Mia stopped, a sudden trepidation replacing her anger, her body tensing.

"I'm going to do whatever I want, honey."

He pulled her skirt up to reveal her perfect, round ass clad in sheer white stockings. Curling his fingers into the waistband, he pulled them down her thighs.

Holy fucking Christ. His cock jerked into full hardness at the sight of her tight full-lace panties. The red lace hugged her hips and disappeared between her soft thighs, a heart-shaped cutout at the back exposing the pale curves of her ass and tempting cleft. Straps crisscrossed the opening and plumped up her cheeks, making him want to sink his teeth into the tantalizing stripes of skin.

Mia had gone still when he pulled up her skirt. Now she twisted to look at him, a small smile on her lips and her eyes darkening with heat.

"Surprise," she murmured.

Gavin let out his breath in a long rush. His cock was throbbing hard enough now that it was impossible to ignore. He was quickly losing control of this situation, if he'd ever had any to begin with.

"You little tease," he said roughly.

"Told you I came here to spend the night. I just bought these today so I could wear them for *you*." Mia wiggled again, her belly pressing against his dick. She sucked in a breath. "My god, Gavin. You're...you get hard so fast..."

He didn't have to touch her cunt to know she was already wet, but he did anyway. He slid his fingers underneath the lace and found her slick heat, the tight little button of her clit. Lust fired through him.

Mia moaned, wiggling her hips like she wanted him to put his fingers inside her. He took his hand away and rested his palm on her ass. She stilled again.

"What...what are you going to do?" she asked, her voice infused with wariness.

"This." He lifted his hand, landing it on her rear with a spank hard enough to sting.

"Ow." Mia flipped her hair away from her face, turning to glower at him. "That hurt."

"No, it didn't. But this one will."

He spanked her again, harder. Mia gasped, her body jerking forward.

"Ow!" she snapped.

"I can make it hurt worse," Gavin said mildly, admiring the pink stain already spreading over the heart-shaped expanse of skin revealed by her panties.

"I believe you," Mia retorted. "You don't have to prove...*ouch!* Son of a..."

She bit off the words, her teeth coming down on her lower lip. He tugged her panties down around her thighs, his blood pulsing in reaction to her naked ass and the secret, glistening folds between her legs. He stroked one finger over her slit before lifting his hand to land another blow on her rear.

"Look, I'm sorry, okay?" Mia squirmed from side to side, trying to escape his hold. "I won't do it again."

"Won't do what again?" He landed another blow, his hand leaving a red imprint on her white cheeks. She yelped.

"Argue with you." Her fingers curled into the carpet, seeking a hold.

Spank.

"What else?"

"Call you names."

Spank.

"What else?"

Mia groaned. "Do things you say are unsafe."

"Good girl."

He stroked his hand over her ass before gripping her waist and lifting her to a sitting position. Her face was flushed with anger, her chest heaving with the force of her breath. She glowered at him, but made no move to either escape his grip or snap at him.

Her stockings and panties were still down around her thighs. He stroked his hand between her legs, dipping one finger into her cunt, damp and swollen with arousal. Mia's breath escaped on a moan as she fisted her hand in his shirt. His erection pushed against her warm, reddened ass, separated only by the thin cotton of his pajama bottoms.

"So that's what happens when I don't do what you say, huh?" She settled against his chest with a sigh, parting her legs as far as she could with the constriction of her panties.

"Does it scare you?" He needed her to say yes.

"Not at all." She pressed her lips to his neck, a smile in her voice. "It made me nervous, but I figured you were into that kind of control thing. I like it, too."

His chest tightened. "You deserve better."

"Oh, stop." She lifted her head to look at him, a trace of frustration rising to her green eyes. "I want to be with you, Gavin. I've been wanting it desperately for over a year. And you're proving to be so much more than I ever could have imagined. Not to mention, you finger my pussy like it's your favorite job."

"It is."

Mia laughed and slid her mouth to his jaw, her body arching against his chest.

"I need you," she whispered, working her hand downward to find the ridge of his cock. "That spanking made me so hot. Please fuck me now."

Nothing in the world could have made him resist that plea. Lifting her into his arms, he strode into the bedroom and lowered her to the bed. With a groan of surrender, he grabbed her hair in his fist, tilted her head back, and brought his mouth down on hers.

Lust and light exploded through him, pooling heat in his groin. Her lips parted, her tongue swept against his, her body quivered. She arched against him as if he were her only secure element, and she moved her hands up to grip his shoulders.

He broke the kiss only so he could move back to pull off her stockings and those ridiculous, sexy little panties. He dropped them to the floor and parted her legs, his dick throbbing at the sight of her spread, pink folds glistening with arousal.

"Hurry." She sat up long enough to pull her dress over her head, revealing a red lace bra with little heart-shaped holes at the front exposing her stiff pink nipples.

"Fuck." He couldn't think of another word past the lust fogging his brain. He sat back to stare at her.

"Also for you." Mia smiled and twisted her nipples through the holes. "I'm on a mission to make you like surprises."

"Best surprise of my life," he muttered, bracing his hands on either side of her head as he leaned in to kiss her.

She made a noise in the back of her throat, skimming her fingers over the bulge in his pants. He drove his tongue into her mouth, a hard possessive desire to own her rising like a tidal wave.

Part of him was aware that despite his display of control, he'd lost the battle. He was smothering every single instinct for her safety—from him, from any threat, from the whole damned world—because he was a selfish bastard who couldn't get enough of her. He wanted to drown in her sweetness, fill himself up with her until she'd obliterated all his darkness.

She sat up, pressing back on his shoulders to encourage him to lie back. He didn't like being the passive one, but she was looking at him with such simmering heat and anticipation that he couldn't disappoint her. He rolled to stretch out on his back. She knelt beside him, smiling as she pulled off his T-shirt and stroked her hands all over his chest.

"You're so hard everywhere," she murmured in wonder, her fingers tracing the ridges of his abdomen before slipping lower to his groin. "Hard, controlling, rigid, authoritarian. Everything I'm not. That's just one of the things I love about us together. Being opposites is what makes us so good."

Love. Good.

No other words in the English language came close to describing all that Mia was. He drove his hand into her hair, brushed his fingers against her soft cheek. He didn't know what to do with everything she made him feel.

She pressed kisses up his neck to his mouth, leaving a trail of fire. He took a breath, restraining himself from rolling her over and plundering her mouth with his. She hooked her fingers into his pants and pulled them off, tossing them to the floor before closing her fingers around his shaft. Heat bolted through him.

"Tell me how you like it," she whispered, swiping her thumb over the head of his cock.

"You're doing it exactly right." He shifted with a wince, pressure tightening his groin. "You can't do anything wrong."

Her laugh was muffled against his chest. "You just spanked me for doing something *wrong*. But I liked it so much I might want to do something wrong again. Except *this* I want to get exactly right."

He reached down to still her hand. "You have it right, honey. So right I'll shoot all over unless you slow down."

A smile curved her mouth. She stretched one leg over him and straddled his waist. With her nipples poking out of her bra, her skin flushed and her hair a waterfall of gold, he could have stared at her for hours if he weren't about to implode with lust. He pinched her rosy nipples and twisted the strap of her bra.

"Take this off," he ordered. "I want you naked."

She shed her bra, revealing her perfect round breasts. She braced her hands on the mattress and leaned in to kiss him deeply, her tongue tracing the line of his lips. He slid his hands down to grasp her ass, working one finger between her cheeks. She inhaled sharply, but didn't protest, arching her back like she wanted more.

He'd give her *more*. And despite her willingness, it might be more than she could handle. More than she could take.

"Wait," she whispered, wiggling back so she was straddling his thighs. "Where are the condoms?"

"Drawer in the nightstand."

She reached over to retrieve one and took her sweet time sheathing his dick. By the time she was done, his teeth were clenched from the light, tickling touch of her fingers.

He grasped her hips. "Ride me."

Mia bit her lip, a flush rising to her cheekbones. For a second he thought she'd decline, but she lifted herself up, her hand circling the base of his cock as she positioned herself.

Then she sank onto him, and the world exploded into the hot, tight clench of her pussy, the sound of her low groan, the clench of her knees around his hips. A flash of pain crossed her face before it was replaced with heavy lust. Heat sizzled through the air. She curled her fingers into his chest and started to move.

"Oh my god." Her breath grew fast, her astonished gaze still holding his. "I feel you so deep, all the way up here."

She pressed one hand to her belly and shifted again, working her gorgeous body up and down on his cock. He dug his fingers into her hips. His jaw clenched to the point of pain. He fought the urge to thrust, to drive them both to the edge. She was a fucking goddess, her tits bouncing, her body flexing and writhing, sweat glistening on her skin.

"Faster." He bit out the order, his blood on fire.

She leaned forward, her hair falling in curtains on either side of her face, her little panting breaths puffing against his neck. Her eyes darkened with hunger and urgency.

"I need it, Gavin," she whispered, her teeth capturing her lower lip again. "I need to come with you inside me, hard and deep and...oh god..."

"That's right." He grabbed her waist and thrust upward, needing to be inside her as far as he could. "Get yourself off... Christ, you're incredible, all soft tight heat...you're going to jerk me off, cover your little pussy with my come..."

A shudder rocked through her. She braced her hands on his chest and moved faster. Breathy cries came from her parted lips.

"I want you to do it first," she gasped, sliding up and down his cock like a well-oiled piston. "Mark me."

She moved off him before he could stop her, her chest heaving as she slid back to sit on his thighs. She rolled the condom off his erection and stroked, her tapered fingers moving up and down his aching shaft, her thumb caressing the swollen crown.

"Do it, Gavin." Her voice was husky and threaded with anticipation. "Come on my pussy. Give me everything you have."

"Ah, shit." Every part of him tensed. Fiery pressure built. He gripped her smooth thighs and thrust into her fist. "So goddamned close...harder...now...*fuck*."

Heat exploded through him, jets of come splashing over her belly, onto her cunt. She gasped, her fist still working his dick until the sensations ebbed. He groaned and sank against the pillows.

"That's so fucking sexy," she whispered, releasing him only to slide her fingers through the mess coating her skin. "I love how you feel on me."

"Get yourself off for me." He stroked his hands up and down her smooth, damp thighs. "I want to watch you."

Shivering, she slipped one hand between her legs and brought the other to her breasts. She twisted her pink nipple and worked her fingers on her clit. Much as he wanted to delve his fingers into her heat again, he restrained himself from reaching for her.

He couldn't take his eyes off the sight of her touching herself, her body sleek and soft. She threw her head back, her hair spilling over her shoulders. Moaning, she moved her fingers more frantically, her body tensing with need.

"Gavin," she gasped. "I feel it...I still feel *you*...oh god, I'm going to...ah!"

A high, keening cry broke from her throat as her body shook, her hand still rubbing her clit. Fucking gorgeous sight, spearing him with fresh lust.

"Oh fuck." She groaned, collapsing on top of him in a hot, sweet bundle of softness. "That was amazing. My ass is still sore from your hand, and I swear that made me come even harder."

He gave a short laugh. Yeah, he'd lost the battle all right. He was about to lose the whole fucking war. And never before had he wanted to surrender.

CHAPTER 13

*a*s their breathing slowed, Gavin twisted a few locks of Mia's hair around his fingers, liking how the golden strands shone in the light. She shifted and slid her hand over his sweaty chest, pressing a kiss against his shoulder.

"Don't move," she murmured. "I'll get dessert."

"You are my dessert."

"This is just as good." She kissed him again before climbing off the bed and hurrying to the kitchen.

He watched her go, admiring the swing of her hips, the bounce of her bare ass. He shifted to the edge of the bed to discard the condom and pull on his pajama pants. Mia returned with a white bakery box and climbed onto the bed again.

"You know I'm devoutly loyal to Polly and Wild Child, but she doesn't make whoopie pies, and they're one of my favorites." She set the box on the nightstand. "Granny used to make them all the time. A few years ago, I found a bakery up in Santa Cruz that makes really yummy whoopie pies. I went up to get a few because I wanted you to try them. I'm also on a mission to get you to love sugar."

She opened the box to reveal a dozen cream-filled pies wrapped in wax paper. Gavin accepted the one she held out to him and moved to sit back on the bed. He didn't even try to understand how his life had gone from eighteen-hour work days and strict routines to whoopie pies and explosive sex with a beautiful girl who'd stepped right out of fairyland.

"The bakery has a ton of different flavors, but I like the originals best." Still gorgeously naked, Mia curled up with her back to the headboard and bit into her pie. "Granny used to make them with French buttercream. It was her go-to treat for whenever I had friends over. Whoopie pies and cold milk."

He took a bite of the pie, appreciating the chocolate, creamy taste but more enamored of the girl sitting beside him. Mia ate with both enjoyment and pure sensuality, slowly relishing each bite, licking her lips and fingers. A fucking miracle that he'd somehow kept her at bay for so long, when now he craved her like an addiction.

"The bakery makes pumpkin whoopie pies in the fall." Mia sucked a drop of cream off her thumb. "They also have a raspberry cream, mint-chip, and red velvet. I think they just launched a lemon one, too."

Gavin's gaze slid to her as she devoured the pastry, licking up the cream and getting chocolate on her lips. She was killing him. He couldn't imagine a better way to go.

"Give me that." He grabbed the whoopie pie from her and leaned over to crush a kiss against her sugary lips. "I'm getting jealous of a damned whoopie pie."

"Hmm." She licked his lower lip. "Maybe I'll learn some new techniques."

Much as he wanted her to demonstrate those techniques on him, Gavin had another idea. He set her half-eaten pie back in the box.

"Lie down," he ordered.

"I wanted to finish that," Mia complained, even as she stretched out against the pillows, her body shifting with the grace of a feline.

"You can have it when I'm done." He shot her a pointed look. "If you're good."

Heat rose to her cheeks. "I will be."

He separated the two cake layers of his whoopie pie and put them in the box, then gathered the pastry cream on his fingers. Mia watched him, her eyes lighting with curiosity and a little nervousness.

"What…" Her pink tongue darted out to lick her lips. "What are you going to do?"

"Spread your pretty legs and you'll find out."

Her breath caught. She spread her legs, exposing her damp pussy, still flushed and swollen from the friction of his cock. He knelt between her legs, raking his gaze over her naked body, the red marks on her hips and thighs evidence of his grip.

He reached over with his other hand to caress her tits. Her nipples were hard again, sticking straight up like little rosebuds. Fuck, but she was perfect.

"You can touch your tits, but nothing else," he said. "Got it?"

Her throat worked with a swallow. "Yes."

Gavin pushed her thighs farther apart and stroked the vanilla cream over her pussy. She flinched at the coldness and gave a breathless laugh.

"What would the baker say about you desecrating his whoopie pie like this?" she asked.

"He'd probably approve." He eased onto his stomach, pressing a kiss to her naval before slowly moving lower.

She tensed, her thigh muscles stiffening. "Gavin. I don't usually let…" Her voice trailed off.

He lifted his head. She watched him, her eyes dark and uncertain.

"You need me to stop?" he asked.

She took a breath. "No. I mean, I don't think so. But..."

"You trust me." It wasn't a question.

"Of course I do."

"Then you know I'll stop if you tell me to."

"Okay."

She was still tense when he pressed a kiss to her inner thigh, inhaling the salty musk of her scent mixed with the cream. He touched his tongue to her clit. She gasped, her hips arching upward. He put his hands on her hipbones to keep her still, licking the cream off, his blood firing at the sweet taste of her.

"Oh my god, Gavin." Her hands fisted in the bedcovers. "That feels incredible."

"Good." He flicked his tongue around her folds and lower.

"Gavin..." She started to pant, twisting her hips and squirming like she wanted him to fuck her with his tongue. "How is it possible that I'm already aroused again...*god*..."

With a muffled grunt of satisfaction, he pressed his fingers to open her before thrusting his tongue inside. She shrieked, one hand tangling in his hair. He shoved his hands under her thighs, spreading them open as the taste, scent, and feel of her flooded every part of him.

He sensed the urgency winding through her, the hot pain of needing relief. He slipped one finger inside her, groaning at the sensation of her tightness, and closed his lips around her clit. She came with a scream, her body vibrating, her fingers yanking his hair. He held her to the mattress, swiping his tongue over her folds as she slid down the other side.

Slowly he eased away from her, bringing her legs together, his veins burning with the force of his own revived lust. Mia didn't move, her chest heaving. She lay with her hands pressed to her eyes, her hands covering her face. Her body shook with what looked like a sob.

Alarm shot through him.

"Mia?" Gavin moved up to the bed to her side, grabbing her wrists.

He pulled her hands away from her face. Tears trickled from her eyes, sliding down her reddened cheeks.

Shit shit shit.

"What?" He rested his hand against the side of her neck, his forehead creasing. "Baby, what's wrong?"

"N-nothing." Her breath hitched. She rolled to her side, curling against him, her head on his chest. "I just...I've never felt like this before. So *safe*, like I can do anything at all. Like I could go out bungee-jumping or sky diving, and everything would be fine because I'd end up right in your arms.

"You make me feel so capable and strong...which is such a stupid thing to say after you just went down on me with a whoopie pie, but I've been so stuck ever since Granny died. I feel like I've been hiding behind this persona of the fun, flirty girl—I mean, I *am* that girl, and I like who I am, but there's so much more to me than that. And you, Gavin Knight, make me believe in all the other parts of who I am."

A red-gold wave swelled underneath his heart. He couldn't, wouldn't, put a name to the feeling, but it filled his veins with light and made him invincible.

He stroked Mia's hair away from her face, letting the long strands slide through his fingers, studying them in the dim light. He'd been wrong to think her hair was just blond or even gold. Like her, it was a thousand honeyed shades—daffodils, flax, butterscotch, amber, lemon, sunshine.

"You deserve to believe in yourself." His voice was rough. Mia deserved so much more than even that. She deserved everything. He wished with all that he was he could be the man to give her *everything*.

She nestled into him with a sigh, her body relaxing. Gavin edged off the bed and eased his arm under her thighs and the

other around her shoulders. After picking her up, he walked to
the bathroom and set her gently in the granite shower stall.

Much as he liked her messy and drenched with lust, he turned
the hot water on and adjusted the temperature. He indicated that
she should get under the spray.

"Are you coming in with me?" She closed her eyes and tilted
her face to the water.

"If I do, you'll come out dirtier, not clean."

"I'd be okay with that," she remarked, even as she sighed with
pleasure when he turned the water hotter.

He was tempted to wash her, wanting to feel the slick, soapy
glide of her skin under his hands, but he didn't trust himself not
to leave her alone. Already his mind blistered with images of
pushing her up against the tile wall, her ass arching toward him...

He closed the shower door, picking up the box of whoopie
pies before returning to the kitchen. He set her half-eaten pie and
another whole one on a plate and leaned against the counter. His
mind filled with images of her in the shower, water sluicing over
her body, her hands soaping her breasts, her thighs and lips
parted.

Sweet and soft though she was, she had a raw lust he craved,
like a cherry soaked in bourbon. He could become obsessed with
her. Probably he already was.

"That was awesome." She came into the kitchen wearing one
of his T-shirts, her legs bare and her wet hair hanging down her
back. "Thank you."

He nodded to the plate waiting for her on the counter and
opened the fridge to take out the milk. Mia made a little noise of
pleasure as she hitched herself onto a stool and bit into her pie.

"So good," she said.

Gavin poured a glass of milk and set it in front of her. "I'm
taking you home after you're done."

She stilled, her expression shadowing. "Why?"

After some consideration, he decided not to tell her about the threatening letter and photos. He needed her to be careful, but he didn't want her to panic right before the wedding—much less at the actual event, which she was so looking forward to. The last thing he wanted was her joy over her friend's wedding to be discolored by fear.

"You need to trust me when I tell you it's best for you to stay at home," he finally said.

She looked down at her plate. "What are you not telling me?"

"Nothing you need to know." He moved closer to her, pushing a lock of her wet hair away from her neck. "If there is something you need to know, I promise I'll tell you. Right now I just need to keep you and everyone else safe, and to make sure the wedding goes without a hitch. I can't do that if you fight me."

She pursed her lips, then nodded. "Okay. But I might get a little scrappy *after* the wedding. All that pent-up frustration, you know."

"I'll look forward to that." He brushed his thumb across her cheek, suppressing his unease over the idea of *after the wedding*. "I'll take you home as soon as you're done."

"I can drive myself."

"You're not driving home alone at this time of night." He put a hard note in his voice to warn her this wasn't up for discussion. "No arguments."

A brief defiance flashed in her eyes, but she turned her attention back to the pies. After finishing both with delighted murmurs that had his dick twitching again, Mia returned to the bedroom to dress. Gavin pulled on jeans and a T-shirt, and they went out to his SUV.

"Polly told me Luke invited you to the family barbeque tomorrow night." Mia pulled her seatbelt on. "She also said you told him you'll be working."

"That's correct." He backed out of the driveway and headed toward Indigo Bay.

"I'll be there," she said. "I'd love it if you took a break and stopped by."

Gavin tightened his fingers on the steering wheel. He hadn't given much thought to socializing in public with Mia. He could control his reactions to her around other people, but it would take an effort he didn't want to expend. And part of him didn't even want to hide. He wanted to claim her as his, to let everyone know she belonged to him.

Then what?

He hated the idea of his life returning to what it had been before Mia had flown into it with her sweet nature and lusty side. But he couldn't give her a hearts-and-flowers future.

"I'm too busy," he said. "The wedding is in a week."

"Can't you spare an hour?" She sounded hurt.

He hardened his heart. "No."

Mia let out her breath in exasperation. "Do you ever socialize with the Stone brothers anymore?"

"Not much."

"Even though you once wanted to be part of their family?"

Gavin flexed his hands on the wheel, not liking where this was going. "Forget it, Mia."

"I won't forget it." She turned to face him. "I hate that you close yourself off from people so much. That's what you did with me, isn't it? Even though you've *noticed* me for a full year."

Gavin pulled into the parking lot of her apartment building and got out, shutting the door to avoid further conversation. As if that was enough to stop her.

"You don't have to live like that anymore." Mia hurried to catch up with him as he strode to the front door. "You don't have to be trapped."

"I know."

"You don't know." Her voice rose. She stabbed the elevator button with her forefinger, her shoulders tight. "You've been trapped in one way or another your whole life. And then you told me that I trapped you. That was never what I wanted. It's certainly not how I feel about you. But if that's what you think this *thing* between us is, then maybe you should reconsider what you want."

His jaw clenched. What he *wanted*, now more than ever, was for this lovely girl to be happy forever. He wanted her to find her heart's desire, to follow it, to live by her granny's dictates about beauty and hope. He wanted her to wear pretty dresses, to laugh and socialize and eat ice cream for dinner.

But how the fuck could she do any of that with him barking orders at her and forcing her into his rigid life?

"You're better off without me," he said. "We both know it."

"Oh, don't give me that crap," Mia snapped. "I may not have everything figured out yet, but I still *choose* to be happy, just like I chose you. I haven't spent all these months trying to get your attention, and finally having it, to let you push me away now."

He had no response to that. Mia approached, sliding her warm hand against the back of his neck.

"I like cupcakes and fairies," she said. "I like having fun. I like stuffed animals, going home, being with my friends. Anything that gives me a warm, fuzzy feeling inside. And every time I saw you at Wild Child, *you* gave me that feeling. You still do. You make me happy."

He wrapped his hand around her wrist and tugged her closer. Breathed her in. Something shifted inside him, like a taut wire relaxing.

"Please come to the barbeque tomorrow." She stood on tiptoe to kiss his nose. "The Stones want you there. Show up and surprise them."

Gavin let out his breath, suddenly blindsided by how fast Mia had gotten under his skin, to the point that his perspective of the world was starting to shift. How bad could things be when there were wildflower wedding bouquets and whoopie pies? Spontaneity could be fun. Following your heart was important. And sometimes, surprises were amazing.

He stepped back from her door, deflecting a sudden painful stab to his chest.

"Get some sleep, sweetheart," he said.

He turned and walked away, feeling her gaze on him as potent as a touch. No matter what happened between them, his life—*he*—would never be the same again.

That might be the biggest surprise of all.

CHAPTER 14

Colorful bouquets of helium balloons rose from the redwood deck railing. More balloons floated from the numerous beribboned posts scattered around the backyard of Warren Stone's vast estate.

The deck stretched out over a manicured lawn that swept down to a magnificent view of the valley. A few dozen people were busy laughing, talking, and playing lawn games. Music floated from a speaker system, and Warren presided over an elaborate grill smoking with the tantalizing smell of steaks and hamburgers.

Under any other circumstance, Mia would have been having a good time—except the party had been underway for well over an hour, and Gavin hadn't shown up. Clearly, despite her impassioned plea, he wasn't going to.

She tried to smother her disappointment, which unfortunately felt more vast and all-encompassing than it should have. Gavin was under siege with security issues, so it was no wonder he didn't have time to attend a family barbeque. Even though it was Saturday, he'd probably been at the office all day or at the wedding villa going over all his checkpoints and whatnot.

Mia had no reason to feel as if his absence was some sort of message about the disparity of their lives—while he worked, she went to parties. He was responsible and grown-up; she was flaky and immature. He needed to spank her when she got sassy (okay, that one totally worked for her). But they could never sustain a long-term relationship. They were night and day, oil and water, fire and ice.

She wanted to tear up that *message* and throw it away.

She gazed at the crowd of people out on the lawn. Polly was engaged in a hula-hooping contest with a group of kids, and her sister Hannah was playing croquet. Evan Stone, who had made a remarkable recovery from a heart surgery that had almost put an end to his and Hannah's budding relationship, was tossing a football with the twins Spencer and Carson. It was all so friendly and homey—exactly the kind of big family gathering that one would want.

And maybe Mia was just feeling morose and a bit lonely, but she was sharply aware of the energy crackling between the couples-in-love. Even though Hannah and Evan were clear across the lawn from each other, an invisible thread seemed to bind them together, causing them both to glance up every so often and catch the other's eye.

And Luke and Polly...well, the love and adoration between them was strong enough to be tangible. Mia had never seen her friend look so glowing and downright *content*, as if all the pieces of her life had finally fit together in the exact right way.

"Uh oh, I see a problem."

She looked up from her place at one of the round tables lining the deck. Adam Stone, the third in line to the Sugar Rush Candy Company throne, was standing beside her and shaking his head in dismay.

"What problem?" she asked.

"Empty glass." He picked up her glass and gave her a wink. "Lucky for you, I can solve that problem. What're you drinking?"

"It was cherry sangria, but I don't need another, thanks."

His expression shifted into a frown, and he pulled out the chair beside her.

"Looks like you need something to cheer you up," he remarked. "Why so glum, chum?"

Mia smiled in spite of herself. She liked all the Stone brothers, but she had a particular affinity for Adam with his tanned, chiseled features, blue eyes, and sun-streaked blond hair that enhanced his easygoing personality.

She'd always envied him a bit—he worked for Sugar Rush as part of Evan Stone's Cocoa Bean Team, visiting farms and plantations in South America and Africa to ensure fair trade and sustainable practices, but he also owned a travel company known for its adventurous trips from African safaris to hiking up a volcano.

In Mia's eyes, Adam Stone was a man who'd figured out early on exactly how to do what he loved. He was also a magnet for female attention, but gorgeous though he was, his surfer-boy looks had never appealed to Mia *in that way*. Not to mention, he was constantly on the move, like he couldn't bear to stay in one place for very long. And while Mia admired his adventuresome spirit, she'd definitely grown roots in Indigo Bay.

"Really," Adam said. "My dad sees you sitting here looking like you lost your best friend, he's going to feel like the whole party is a failure."

"I'm fine," she assured him. "I was just thinking about the wedding. Have all the groomsmen gotten their final fittings taken care of?"

He groaned. "God, yes. You'd think the king of England was getting married, what with all the fuss going on. I don't know about Tyler, though. He's been bitching and complaining that his tux is too itchy."

Mia smiled again, glancing over to where Tyler Stone, the youngest brother, was flipping burgers next to his father at the grill. Rakishly handsome, he'd once had a well-deserved bad boy reputation before he'd both fallen hard and straightened up for Kate Darling, Luke's super-efficient executive assistant. At the moment, Kate was busy organizing the table of plates, side dishes, and condiments, throwing Tyler amused grins whenever he reached over to pat her on the ass. Which was often.

Mia wished she and Gavin had the kind of relationship where he'd pat her on the ass in public. Heck, she wished he'd even *go out* with her in public.

Lord. She needed to get out of this funk or she'd be drowning herself in cherry sangria before the night was over.

"So, Adam, tell me what you've been up to." She flipped her hair back and forced a breezy, interested tone into her voice. "Still working on the Cocoa Bean Team?"

He nodded, plucking a tortilla chip out of the bowl on the table. "We're working on a big sustainability project down in Venezuela."

"Polly told me about that. Are you leaving town right after the big event?"

"Yeah, the day after. People start arriving next month, so we need to make sure the infrastructure is in place. Students, scientists, Sugar Rush employees. We still have space, if you want to lend a hand."

"Living in a rickety cabin or a tent, sharing an outhouse with ten other people, battling mosquitos the size of garbage trucks?" Mia shook her head. "Sounds delightful, but I'll pass."

Adam grinned. "Not an outdoor girl, huh?"

"Not unless a nice hotel room with running water and a flushable toilet counts as *outdoors*."

"A woman after my own heart." Julia Bennett, the Stone brothers' aunt who'd become the family matriarch after the death of their mother, pulled out a chair beside Adam.

In her mid-forties, Julia was a renowned fashion stylist who needed no other advertising except for her flawlessly elegant appearance. She wore a striped, seersucker shirt and mid-length skirt and had arranged her blond hair into a chignon that managed to look just the right amount of untidy. Understated gold jewelry adorned her arms and neck, and her cosmetics enhanced her fine, princess-like features.

"Warren tells me he's planning to join you the week before the project begins," Julia told Adam. "He can't stay for the duration, but he wants to be there when you're getting things started."

Adam nodded and launched into details about the first week's plans. Mia took the opportunity to study Julia. She'd never had much interaction with the other woman, but she certainly knew a lot about her thanks to Polly, whose relationship with Julia had run the gamut from mortal enemies to BFFs. Julia was sharp, formidable, fiercely loyal to her friends and family, and took no prisoners when she was crossed.

Polly had grown to implicitly trust and rely on Julia's opinion, which gave Mia a bit of courage. After Adam excused himself to help with the food, she moved into the chair beside the older woman.

"Do you mind if I ask your opinion about something?" Mia asked.

Julia peered at her. "Not at all."

Mia took a breath. Worst case scenario, Julia would sniff disdainfully at her idea and tell her not to bother wasting her time. Best case scenario…?

"With all the wedding details, I've learned a lot about event planning." Mia's heartbeat ratcheted up a notch. "I've made numerous contacts, developed efficient organizational systems, and I know how to handle the practicalities of budgeting as well as the creative stuff. So I'm considering starting my own event planning business."

Julia arched an eyebrow. "What do you do now?"

"I work at an insurance agency. It totally sucks."

A faint smile pulled at Julia's mouth. "And you think event planning is easier?"

"No, but it's so much *better*," Mia said. "And since you're kind of in the same field, I wanted to ask what you think of the idea."

"I *know* you'd be competing with much more well-established companies," Julia replied archly. "Including at least three whom I tried to convince Polly to work with. You'd have to work hard to make a name for yourself, though having Luke Stone's wedding on your resume will be a significant advantage. If you establish a good reputation and know how to rise above the competition, you'd likely have no shortage of clients in Indigo Bay."

Some of the tension eased from Mia's chest. At least Julia hadn't laughed at her inexperience.

"If you screw it up, however, you'd be finished," Julia added.

"No pressure then, huh?" Mia asked.

Amusement crossed Julia's face. Mia was about to ask how Julia had gotten started in personal styling when Spencer, Carson, and Polly approached. The tall, dark-haired twins had the exact same features—strong jaws, thick-lashed brown eyes, straight noses—but they were easy to tell apart. A scientist in the Sugar Rush candy laboratories, Spencer wore glasses and had a polite, thoughtful demeanor that added to his hunky-nerd vibe. By contrast, Carson was more easily designated as a corporate VP like his father and older brothers.

"Come on, both of you," Polly said to her and Julia. "We need two more for croquet."

Mia was tempted to decline, but she didn't want to just sit here being depressed about Gavin. She and Julia joined the game, batting the balls through the wickets until Tyler called that dinner was ready.

Mia went into the house to use the bathroom and wash her hands, returning to the deck as guests lined up in front of the grill to choose their steaks and burgers.

A deep voice floated through the air, skimming over her skin like a caress. Mia turned, her heart cartwheeling at the sight of Gavin.

He was here!

She drank him in, tall and unbearably handsome in black trousers and a button-down gray shirt open at the collar to reveal the tanned column of his throat. He was talking to Luke Stone, but his gaze flickered past the other man to stop on her.

She drew in a breath, everything inside her caught in the trap of his blue-eyed gaze. Then he winked at her before turning his attention back to whatever Luke was saying.

Much as she longed to fly across the deck right into Gavin's arms, Mia picked up a plate and began helping herself to the food. Professional and private as he was, Gavin wouldn't want anyone else to know they were a *thing*, so she'd have to keep her PDA urges to herself. That was all right; just knowing he was so close was enough to make her happy.

The guests all began sitting down to eat. Mia joined Polly, Julia, and Spencer back at the table, making small-talk while picking at her food and trying not to search too obviously for Gavin. Only when people finished eating and started back to playing games did she scan the party for him.

He stood talking to a tall, bearded man wearing a baseball cap. To anyone else, Mia suspected they'd look like two men casually chatting during a barbeque, but she noticed the tense set of Gavin's stance.

When he walked away from the conversation, she excused herself from the table and crossed the lawn toward him. He'd paused to watch an in-progress game of horseshoe, his arms crossed over his chest. With his chiseled features, his gray shirt, his ramrod straight bearing, he was like a steel sculpture amidst the laughter and bright helium balloon bouquets.

He turned when she was halfway to him, as if he'd sensed her approach.

"Hi," she said.

His gaze roamed over her floral mini-dress, the lacy hem reaching mid-thigh and the halter-style top leaving her arms and shoulders bare. Even though she hadn't been certain he would show up, she'd worn the dress with him in mind. It seemed she was doing everything with him in mind these days.

"Nice dress," he said, the undercurrent of his voice telling her that he'd like to take it off her right then and there.

"I wore it for you." She reached out and impulsively touched his hand, tilting her head toward a section of the lawn that had been designated as an unofficial dance floor. "Will you dance with me?"

His gaze slanted toward the deck, where people still lingered at the tables. For a heart-stopping moment, she thought he'd decline, but then he took her hand in his and led her to the dance area.

He slipped an arm around her waist, tugging her closer but not too close to be overtly intimate. She breathed in his scent that had become so familiar, reveled in the sensation of his strong arm against her lower back, tightened her hand around his.

"I'm glad you came," she said.

"I'm always glad when you come," he deadpanned.

Mia giggled, giving him a light, chastising slap on the chest. "Careful, or you'll get me revved up right here and now."

He made a rumbling noise in his chest and tugged her closer, his hand sliding from her lower back to the top curve of her ass.

"So why did you decide to make an appearance?" she asked.

"I knew it would make you happy if I did."

Mia blinked. "Really? You're here for me?"

"Everything I do outside of work these days is *for you*." He brushed a lock of hair away from her neck.

Her heart warmed. She glanced over his shoulder to where Polly had paused in a game of kickball to look at them. Her friend smiled, giving Mia a discreet thumb's up before returning to the game.

"Come on, let's get some dessert." Mia slid her hand to Gavin's, tangling their fingers together before leading him to the deck.

Relieved when he didn't pull away from her, she was aware of several glances in their direction as they helped themselves to Wild Child Declairs from the dessert table.

"Hey, Gavin, come here." Spencer Stone waved Gavin over to where a group of men sat drinking beer and talking. "Need you to settle a bet."

Gavin started to shake his head, but Mia gave him a nudge in the side.

"Go," she whispered.

He set his plate on a table and approached the men. Mia sat down, watching as two of the Stone brothers greeted him with manly hugs and back-slaps, drawing him effortlessly into the conversation.

Clearly the Stone family loved Gavin, and yet still he'd been distancing himself from them ever since his return from Iraq. He purposely avoided being close to anyone.

Except slowly, inch by inch, he'd been letting her in. He'd allowed her to see past his inflexible exterior and controlling nature. That was a gift she would not take lightly.

Though she longed to confess that her feelings for him had grown to epic proportions, that he made her heart sing as powerfully as he made her body burn, she had to be careful or risk intensifying his ridiculous notions about not being able to give her what she "deserved."

She returned to the dessert table as Gavin approached.

"What was the bet?" she asked.

"Baseball odds." He skimmed his fingers across her bare arm. "Kate's the one who knows all the details, though, so I told them to ask her. She even keeps spreadsheets."

Mia smiled and made a mental note to talk to the super-organized and efficient Kate about the logistical paperwork needed to start a business.

"Hey, who was that man you were talking to earlier?" She elbowed Gavin and indicated the bearded man who was walking toward the deck.

"The guy who's providing the fireworks." Gavin still didn't sound any too pleased about the idea of surprise fireworks at the wedding.

"You told me everything checked out okay."

"Yeah, but I'm only allowing them because they'll be far enough from the villa. And I'm sending an operative on the boat as an extra security measure."

Mia knew Gavin wouldn't let his guard down until the wedding was over and everyone was safe. She took an enormous amount of comfort in his unyielding protectiveness. Even with a scary threat to the wedding, she had no doubt that everything would be fine. After all, Gavin Knight was in charge.

She examined the multiple dessert plates spread over the table, which contained everything from éclairs to fruit tarts.

"Do you want one?" She plucked a strawberry tart from a tray.

"No." He lowered his mouth closer to her ear and murmured, "I'll get some sugar from you later."

She chuckled, half turning to face him when a loud *bang* split through the air.

Mia startled, dropping the paper plate. Before she could take another breath, Gavin was in front of her, shielding her with his body.

Bang bang bang!

Her heart jumped into her throat. What the—

Gavin backed up, crowding her against the side of the house, his muscles locking. Warren Stone's deep voice rose above the chatter.

"No shooting pebbles, kids!" he shouted. "Not safe."

A bunch of kids grumbled in protest, but the banging noises

stopped. Mia peered around Gavin to where several of the helium balloons attached to the deck had gone flat. Behind them, the group of children dispersed, each of them clutching a straw through which they'd apparently been firing pebbles at the balloons.

Mia gave a weak laugh and rested her hand on Gavin's back. "False alarm."

His shoulders were stiff enough to break. She frowned, running her fingers over his spine.

"You okay?"

He stepped away from her, his jaw tight. Mia's heart sank. With his PTSD and nightmares, sudden noises might incite a flashback or, at the very least, bad memories.

"Gavin..." She reached to touch his arm.

He shook her away and strode toward the house, his back as rigid as metal.

CHAPTER 15

*M*ia bit her lip, uncertain whether or not to go after Gavin. No one seemed to have noticed his reaction to the noise—everyone was back to talking, playing games, and picking out desserts.

She hurried into the house, catching sight of him walking to the foyer.

"Gavin!" Her voice echoed against the stone floor. "Wait."

He took his jacket from a rack and started toward the door. She quickened her pace and grabbed his arm, yanking him to a halt. She almost reeled backward at the look in his eyes—bleak and dark as a black hole. An ache ripped through her.

"I need to go." He pulled away from her.

"Will you drive me home?" Mia asked quickly.

He frowned, deep grooves carved on either side of his mouth. "Didn't you drive here?"

"Yes, but…uh, my car is making a rattling noise," she invented. "I'm not sure it's safe to drive."

"Luke or Polly will give you a ride."

"But they're having such a good time I don't want to bother them."

"So ask one of the other Stones."

"Same thing. Good time. Don't want to interrupt."

Though his eyes hardened to the consistency of granite, he yanked open the front door and ushered her out. Mia grabbed her purse from the foyer table and hurried to the driveway before he could think of some other way for her to get home.

They got into his SUV. Mia texted Polly and Luke, apologizing for the sudden departure and assuring them everything was fine. Tense silence simmered between her and Gavin as he drove to her apartment, his hands so tight on the steering wheel his knuckles turned white. He pulled into a space in her building parking lot, braking hard.

As she'd expected, he exited the SUV to walk her to her door. Mia fished in her purse for her keys, her heartbeat suddenly increasing as she unlocked the door. Though she'd witnessed more of Gavin's angles and layers than she'd ever imagined he possessed, she had no idea how to help him contend with his past trauma. Maybe it was arrogant to even think she could.

"All right." He stepped aside when she entered her apartment. "I'm going back to work."

"Wait." Her hand tightened on the door handle. "Come inside for a while."

He shook his head, but his gaze slanted past her to the frilly, warm interior.

"Gavin." She didn't reach for him again out of fear he might pull away, but she held open the door in invitation and gave him her best beseeching look. "Please come in. Just for a few minutes."

He dragged a hand through his hair with a sigh, but followed her in. Mia closed and locked the door behind him with a surge of triumph. He didn't want anyone, least of all her, to acknowledge his weaknesses so she'd have to tread carefully.

"Sit down." She gestured to the sofa.

He sat, the tense lines of his body easing slightly. Mia went into the kitchen and opened the cupboards. She didn't have any of the hard liquor he favored, so she poured a glass of wine and brought it to him.

He eyed the glass with suspicion. "What's this?"

"Wine."

"It's pink."

"It's rosé." When he looked blank, she added, "A combination of red and white."

"I know what rosé is."

"So drink it, tough guy."

He scowled, but took a swallow before setting the glass on the coffee table. Maybe she should have offered him ice cream instead. She pulled an ottoman closer to him and sat, resting her elbows on her knees.

"Can I get you anything else?" she asked.

He shook his head. Frustration nudged at her. He took care of her so well, like he didn't even have to think to know what would make her feel better, and yet when the tables were turned all she could manage to give him was a glass of pink wine.

She leaned down to take off his shoes and lifted his feet onto the ottoman. When she knelt beside him on the sofa, a gleam of interest replaced the scowly, suspicious look in his eyes.

"We're not doing that." She pushed him backward so he was sitting against the sofa pillows.

Any other man would have looked ridiculous against the frilly heart-shaped pillows and stuffed animals, but Gavin was even more masculine than usual—if that was possible—his dark hair and hard-edged features a striking contrast to the feminine background.

Mia took off his suit jacket and loosened his belt. She purposely avoided brushing against the bulge in his trousers, even when he tried to lift up her skirt.

"Stop that." She swatted his hand away.

"Are you wearing underwear?"

"Good lord. I'd never go commando in a skirt this short. What kind of girl do you think I am?"

"The sugar, spice, and everything nice kind." He ran his hand over her bare thigh.

"*Stop* that." She wiggled off the sofa, picking up the glass of rosé before returning to the kitchen. She made a cup of hot cocoa, added multicolored marshmallows, and brought it to Gavin.

He frowned. Of course he *frowned*. He'd probably never had a nice hot cup of cocoa in his life, poor man. Probably he didn't even know what it was.

"It's much better than pink wine," Mia assured him, setting the mug on the table beside him. "You just sit right there and relax."

"Are you going to do a striptease?"

"Save that thought for another day." She smirked at him. "I'm actually going to give you my granny's brand of medicine. She always made me a cup of hot cocoa when I was having a bad day."

As she'd expected, the mention of Granny extinguished the brewing lust in Gavin's eyes. He picked up the mug and studied the melting marshmallows before taking a sip. He grunted a noise of approval.

"Right?" Mia said proudly. "Made from scratch with real cocoa powder and a touch of cinnamon."

She turned her music player to a new-age station with slow, peaceful sounds of echoing waterfalls and ocean waves. She fetched a box and a lap desk from the bookshelf and returned to sit beside him. "So like I told you, Granny was an artist. One of the things she did was illustrate coloring books for grown-ups."

"Why do grown-ups need coloring books?"

"You haven't heard of the phenomenon? Coloring is excellent for stress relief and meditation, so tons of people are doing it now. Granny's books were all about enchanted forests and lands where elves and fairies live. She'd always ask me to test drive her illustrations before publication by coloring them in so she could see if she wanted to make any changes. Some of my best memories are sitting in the kitchen with her, drinking hot cocoa and coloring the pictures she'd drawn."

Feeling his gaze on her, curious and intent, Mia lifted the lid of the box and took out several of Granny's paperback coloring books. A set of fine-point markers rested at the bottom of the box. She bustled around for a minute, setting the desk on Gavin's lap and selecting a double-page spread of a forest grove filled with hollow trees surrounding a lantern-lit elven village.

"What am I supposed to do with this?" He frowned, getting scowly again.

"Color it, genius." Mia placed the markers into a pouch at the side of the desk. "Come on, I'll do it with you. You take that page, and I'll take this one."

She eased closer to him, edging the desk partway onto her lap and trying not to be distracted by the sensation of his muscular thigh pressing against hers and the delicious scent of his shaving cream drifting to her nose.

She cleared her throat and tried to focus. "Granny would always write a story accompanying the illustrations, but she never included it in the coloring books since she wanted people to create their own narrative. If you look carefully, though, you can see the story in the pictures. This one is about an elf girl of humble origins who enlists the help of woodland creatures to help her find a magic pendant that will save the forest from destruction."

She plucked the cap from a marker and started coloring the heart-shaped leaves of a tree. Gavin watched her and drank his hot cocoa, and for a few minutes she thought there was no way he'd actually *color*. Then he set the mug down and picked up a marker.

Mia wanted to cheer. She settled against the pillows, relieved he was not only making an effort but hadn't scoffed and left her apartment to go back to work. She switched her marker for a light green and continued coloring the tree, glancing over only occasionally to check Gavin's progress.

Of course his technique was intensely precise and inside the lines, but he was coloring a mushroom cluster with purple, then filling in the little dots with bright yellow.

As they worked for the next hour, he colored his half of the forest with all shades of blue, lavender, peach, orange, and coral. He gave the elven girls rainbow skirts and polka-dot shirts, and he turned the sky into an expanse of cotton candy with fluffy pink clouds.

Mia was enchanted, especially as she'd expected him to infuse the forest with realistic browns and dark green—if he colored at all. And not only was he coloring, he was creating a vivid, lovely dreamland that would have made Granny very happy.

"Why are you smiling?" He glanced sideways at her from behind his glasses, but the lines of stress had faded from his face.

"I like it." She tilted her head to the illustration. "It's whimsical. I didn't think you did whimsical."

"I don't." He squinted and filled in the twigs of a bird's nest with alternating purple and fuchsia. "This is for you."

Her insides did a little flip. "What do you mean, it's for me?"

He took out a blue marker to color the bird, his expression grave with concentration. "It's the kind of forest you'd live in, my little fairy girl."

Mia hadn't known until that moment that it was possible for her heart to smile from ear to ear.

"Aw." She nudged his hip with hers. "That's really sweet."

"I know." He colored each individual feather of the bird's wings.

Still smiling, Mia settled back in to coloring her side of the forest. With the soothing music drifting through the air alongside the smell of chocolate, and Gavin's body so strong and solid beside hers, she couldn't help imagining what it would be like to spend all of her evenings like this.

Well, *some* of her evenings, in-between seeking out new, cozy little restaurants where she and Gavin could have dinner, or going to the movies with him, or meeting him at one of her favorite haunts for a drink, or picking up Indian takeout for them on the way home, or strolling hand-in-hand along the beach at sunset…

Longing filled her, a rush so hard and fast it almost took her breath away.

"You okay?" Gavin peered at her, as if he'd sensed the sudden shift in her.

Of course he had. He was so attuned to her he noticed every subtle change in her mood. But did he know that she was falling in love with him?

A wild combination of joy and apprehension surged through her. She set her marker down and snuggled up against his side, resting her head on his shoulder.

"What's going on?" He settled his hand on her thigh.

"Nothing." She rubbed her cheek against his shoulder. "I just have it bad for you, Gavin Knight. I've had it bad for you for over a year."

"Hmm." His voice rumbled in his chest. "I don't feel the same way."

The smile faded from her heart. "You don't?"

"No." He slipped his hand under her chin, lifting her face to look at him.

Behind his glasses, his eyes were warm and tender—whatever past trauma or fear he'd experienced at the barbeque was gone. Mia took some comfort in the fact that her brand of medicine had worked—hot cocoa and coloring had soothed his pain.

"I don't have it bad for you, Mia Donovan." He brushed his thumb across her cheek. "But I do have it *good* for you. Better than I could ever have imagined."

He lowered his mouth to hers. And in that moment, she believed it was true, that her world of cupcakes and pink lace was a perfect match for his world of strict security and control. Because right between those two worlds, like the overlapping circles of a Venn diagram, was the enchanted forest where they both could live.

Together.

CHAPTER 16

"Oh, Polly." Mia pressed a hand to her chest. "You're beautiful."

Polly smiled. *Beautiful* wasn't the right word. She was radiant in her antique lace sheath dress with cap sleeves and a sweetheart neckline, her hair falling in glossy curls around her face.

Despite the high-profile nature of the wedding, Polly and Mia had ensured plenty of bohemian touches, from the wildflower bouquets to the rustic place settings. But the gown was the most exquisite, fitting Polly's figure to perfection and enhanced by the embroidered veil and the silver pendant that had once belonged to her mother.

"I still can hardly believe it," Polly confessed. "Me? Marrying the CEO of Sugar Rush?"

"Actually, it's the CEO of Sugar Rush marrying *you*," Mia corrected. "He's the one who shouldn't believe his luck."

Polly turned from the mirror. For now, the two of them were alone in the upstairs bedroom of the villa. Afternoon sunlight gleamed through the wrought-iron windows that overlooked the courtyard where the seats were arranged in a semi-circle around the terrace where Luke would be waiting for Polly.

"I'm going to do a final check before the guests arrive." Mia adjusted the short train of Polly's gown. "And I'm guessing Julia will be here any minute to do some last-minute fussing of your hair and makeup."

Polly turned, capturing Mia's hand in hers. "You're the best friend I could ever have hoped for. I don't feel like I've told you that enough, but everything you've done for me...I wouldn't have met Luke if it hadn't been for you."

"Yes, you would have," Mia said. "Destiny can't be thwarted."

"What about *your* destiny?" Polly lifted an eyebrow.

Mia turned away so her friend wouldn't see the flush rising over her cheeks. "What about it?"

"Does it involve Gavin Knight?"

Oh, how Mia hoped that it did. But her feelings for Gavin were bursting through her like shooting stars, so brilliant that she couldn't put them into words.

"Hey." Polly squeezed Mia's hand. "I may be a bridezilla, but I've seen the way he looks at you. And at the barbeque, I thought you two were going to go up in flames right there on the dance floor. So you need to tell me if he's everything you've been hoping he would be."

Mia's throat tightened as she turned to look into her friend's earnest brown eyes. "Polly, he's so much *more* than I hoped for. So much more than I ever dreamed."

Polly smiled, but before she could say anything else, Mia reached up to adjust her veil.

"However," she said firmly, "today is about you and Luke."

"That doesn't change the fact that I want you to be happy."

"I am. Especially for you." Because both she and Polly were starting to get a little teary-eyed, Mia added, "'After all, mawidge and wuv, true wuv, is what bwings us todeger today.'"

Polly laughed and reached for a tissue. Mia had no doubt that her and Luke's marriage would outshine even Westley and Buttercup's romance.

She and Polly exchanged an embrace, and Mia left before either one of them got even weepier and ruined their mascara. The bridesmaids were busy getting ready in the adjoining room, and the groom's party was in the opposite wing of the villa. Luke's five brothers were all serving as his groomsmen, with Evan as best man, and their sister Hailey would be one of Polly's bridesmaids.

Mia went downstairs to ensure everything was running smoothly. Although Lorraine, the villa manager, would be handling the logistics, Mia couldn't help herself from doing a final check.

She started toward the courtyard just as Gavin rounded the corner, looking magnificent in a charcoal-gray suit and silk tie, his dark hair brushed away from his forehead and his glasses emphasizing the strong lines of his face.

Mia's knees weakened at the sight of him. He caught her eye and sent her a solemn wink, then slipped his gaze appreciatively over her body clad in the royal blue silk-and-lace maid of honor gown.

She glanced around quickly to ensure no one else was nearby. Then she hurried toward him and slipped her arms around his waist.

"It's going to be perfect," she whispered.

He smiled, lowering his head to press a kiss against her lips. "You're perfect. But I can't look at you again or you'll distract me from my job."

"I'll save you a dance."

"I'm on duty until the entire event is over and everyone is safe at home." He stepped back and took her hands, giving her a quick, spinning twirl. "But save me a dance for tomorrow, beautiful."

He spun her again, bringing her hand to his lips before letting her go. He crossed the room to the side door, one hand on his earpiece.

All a-tingle, Mia completed her survey of the various rooms. The reception hall was stunning—wildflower arrangements hung from the ceiling over round tables draped with blue linen. Silver bowls of Sugar Rush candy sat in various places, and the Wild Child cake glowed like a jewel at the cake table.

As the sun set, candles and strings of tree lights and lanterns would illuminate the foyer and courtyard. Ceramic pots of colorful flowers lined the entrance to the villa, and trees surrounded the terrace. It was rustic, lovely, and decidedly intimate despite the fact that over three hundred guests were already starting to arrive.

She started back to the stairs just as Lorraine came in the front door, her worried expression fading at the sight of Mia.

"Oh, I'm glad you're here," she said. "Some of the guests are arriving with gifts, and I don't know where to put them."

"Gifts? There aren't supposed to be any gifts. Polly and Luke specifically asked for charity donations instead."

"Well, security is confiscating a bunch of gift-wrapped packages with silver ribbon, and the guests are getting a little upset," Lorraine said. "One of the security guys is piling them over by the trucks, which isn't exactly considerate. I know they won't let packages into the villa, but we can't just let them leave *wedding presents* outside."

"Have you talked to Mr. Knight?" Mia asked.

"I wanted to, but the security guy said he went to supervise the access control at the gate."

Mia sighed. "Let's put them in the front room, I guess. It's not being used for the event, and no, it's not right to leave wedding presents outside. One of the men will let Gavin know when he gets back."

She and Lorraine hurried to transfer the gifts to the front room before Mia realized the ceremony was scheduled to start in less than half an hour. She went back upstairs to help the other bridesmaids and Polly finish getting ready. As it turned out, she needn't have bothered since Julia Bennett was overseeing the women with the aplomb of an orchestra conductor.

Most of the guests had arrived well in advance of the five p.m. ceremony, as if they'd known that the privilege of attending Luke Stone's wedding came with the price of access control. Police officers guided cars into the parking lot, and Gavin's security team patrolled the area with unobtrusive stealth.

The day was finally here. Absorbing Polly's joy, the excitement of the bridesmaids, the jubilant energy…Mia couldn't have been more thrilled that she'd been able to contribute to such a memorable day. And what if she *could* do this as an actual career? She couldn't imagine a better way to create joy and beauty.

Lorraine came to tell them that all the guests were seated, Luke and his brothers were in their places, and the procession was scheduled to begin in ten minutes. A flurry of happy excitement filled the air as the women descended the stairs and lined up outside the foyer door.

Music drifted from the string quartet seated in the courtyard, and Mia peeked around the door to see the groomsmen and Luke entering from the right side to take their places at the terrace. They were an impressive, handsome group of men…but at the moment, all of Luke's younger brothers faded in his bright, captivating glow.

The bridesmaid processional began. Mia stood next to Polly to await her turn. In the absence of both parents, Polly had chosen to walk herself down the aisle, and Mia could see the sudden nervousness rise to her friend's eyes.

She squeezed Polly's hand. "I'll be right there."

"I know. You're the only person I trust to tell me if I have a booger in my nose."

Mia laughed. "You don't. And even if you did, I'd still love you."

"Same here."

Mia did a last-minute check of Polly's train and veil before starting down the aisle herself. The guests were an eclectic bunch—on Luke's side, high-society men and women in designer clothing, and on Polly's side, the hippie crowd from Wild Child in chiffon maxi-dresses and rumpled suits. It could not have been a more perfect representation of Polly and Luke's union.

Murmurs of admiration rose as Polly came down the aisle, though when she and Luke locked gazes, it seemed as if the rest of the room disappeared for them. She took his outstretched hand. He lowered his head and whispered something in her ear that caused a warm smile to bloom over her face.

The ceremony was simple and sweet, the couple exchanging their own vows with such heartfelt emotion that Mia suspected there wasn't a dry eye in the house. Afterward, a flurry of activity took place with photographs and a cocktail hour.

A festive atmosphere filled the villa as the lanterns and lumi-naire cast a warm, amber glow over the reception, and the party began in earnest. There was dancing, toasts, an elaborate sit-down dinner, and plenty of champagne. Mia danced with each Stone brother in turn, as well as Warren Stone, who proved to be the best dancer of them all.

After the cake-cutting, Hannah caught hold of Mia's elbow and tugged her to the side of the room.

"The boat reached its anchor point, so they're ready to start as soon as everyone is outside," she whispered. "The band moved to the outdoor stage when Polly was cutting the cake, so it shouldn't be hard to get everyone out there. I asked Evan to make an announcement."

"I'll help with crowd control, so we don't have any stragglers," Mia said.

Evan picked up the mic to encourage everyone to head outside to the manicured gardens on the perimeter of the villa grounds.

"It's such a beautiful night that we've set up a bar and stage overlooking the ocean," he said. "So let's keep the party going outside."

Voices rose in happy agreement as all the guests filed outside, trailed by laughter and excitement. Mia took the opportunity to detour to the ladies' room. Two men dressed in black suits passed her in the foyer, both with severe expressions.

She ignored the faint unease rising inside her. She'd been decidedly impressed all evening with Gavin's security procedures. Only when she'd caught a glimpse of an earpiece or a man speaking discreetly into a handset had she noticed any evidence of his team.

She used the restroom, taking a few extra minutes to powder her nose before heading back to the foyer. As she passed the bustling kitchen, Lorraine stepped out and gestured frantically to her.

"Did he find you?" she asked.

"Who?"

"Mr. Knight. The security guys at the gate just stopped an unauthorized truck from entering. The delivery guy said he was delivering pizzas for the security team."

"That was Polly's idea," Mia explained. "Gavin wouldn't let her order extra food for his team, so she planned for a pizza delivery halfway through the evening."

"Mr. Knight refused to let them in, and now he's plenty mad there was a planned delivery that he hadn't been told about."

Mia's heart sank. Polly had known the delivery truck needed to stay on the exterior of the security ring so it wouldn't interfere with Gavin's operations.

"I'll find him and explain," she told Lorraine. "Do you know where he is?"

"He was stalking through the courtyard, last I saw him."

Mia thanked her and hurried outside. A few men patrolled the perimeter of the courtyard, but Gavin was nowhere in sight. She went back inside and crossed the foyer to the front entrance.

He was coming up the front steps, the lines of his body tight with tension.

Great. She had to calm him down before anyone at the wedding discovered the chief of security was about to lose it.

She held up a hand as he approached. "Gavin, calm down."

"Why didn't you tell me about the gifts?" he snapped.

"The gifts? I thought you were upset about the pizza."

"I am. I said *no unauthorized deliveries*. Nothing that hasn't been personally cleared by me. I sure as hell didn't get any notice about pizza."

"Polly was worried your men would be hungry, and since you told her not to order extra food for them, she wanted to make sure they had something for dinner."

Gavin muttered a curse, his hands flexing. "Much as I appreciate Polly's concern, my men are here to *work*. We don't eat or take breaks on duty. When did you know about this?"

"Um…" Mia's heart began a slow descent to her stomach. "Yesterday. It was a last-minute idea."

His jaw clenched. "And you didn't tell me?"

"I thought it would be fine if the pizza truck stopped outside the *exterior circle*," she said, her own anger rising alongside a stab of guilt. "I'd never have told them to breach all your security lines. I mean, random members of the public are down on the road waiting for Luke and Polly's departure, so why would it be a big deal if the pizza guy stopped there too?"

"Because I had to go the fuck out there and deal with an unexpected and unexplained issue when I need to be on-site," Gavin snapped, his eyes flashing. "Now I hear there's a bunch of goddamned packages in the front room that you also didn't tell me about. You assured me there would be no gifts."

"There weren't supposed to be," Mia explained. "Polly and Luke requested donations to the Rebecca Stone Foundation in lieu of gifts. It was on the invitation. I had no idea people would actually bring anything, and I hadn't made arrangements for what to do with them. So I put them in the front room."

"*You* put them in the front room?" A muscle ticked in his jaw. "What the hell were you thinking, putting yourself at risk like that?"

Mia couldn't deflect his anger. It speared right into her, blooming hurt through her chest.

"I...I didn't know what else to do," she finally said.

"And why am I just now finding out about this?"

"Because you were out at the *main access point* when the guests were arriving." Mia lifted her chin, forcing a belligerent note into her voice. "And your team was confiscating the presents and leaving them outside, which is terrible wedding etiquette, not to mention disrespectful. So I had to make a decision. If one of your men didn't tell you, don't blame me."

He stared at her with such disbelief that her insides shriveled up.

"You and I worked our asses off to get this event locked down in record time, and yet it didn't occur to you to tell me yourself?" he asked.

Shit. No, it hadn't occurred to her because she'd been too busy helping Polly with her dress, checking the decorations, and getting ready herself, and besides she wasn't supposed to be in charge of anything on the day of the event *anyway*...

No.

Gavin was right. After their contentious start, they'd worked hard *together* to ensure they both got what they wanted for the wedding. Mia had heard his dictates countless times by now, and she'd known perfectly well that she should notify him if anything unexpected occurred.

But she'd failed. Gavin would never have made such a stupid mistake because he was so fucking *good* at the operating instructions of life, whereas her big contribution was color-coordinating napkins and flower arrangements.

And sure they'd ended up partnering well to organize their friends' wedding-of-a-lifetime, but suddenly Mia realized that when the big event was over, she and Gavin would have nothing left in common.

There was no stupid *enchanted forest* where they could live happily ever after. No world where frosted cupcakes would ease his PTSD, and she would decorate his steel security briefcase with stickers of hearts and flowers.

What a fool she was. After the wedding, Gavin would plunge back into work 24/7, tracking security risks with methodical precision, while she'd sit in her cubicle at the insurance agency trying to figure out if she should offer party packages to get her event planning business off the ground.

Oh my god.

She blinked back her tears, stunned that she hadn't seen it before now. She'd been slowly falling in love with Gavin Knight for the past year, but only now did she realize how desperately she wanted to have *more* with him. She wanted him to be her steadying force, the man she came home to, the warrior she'd freed.

And yet it was a wish as futile as wanting Granny back.

"I'm having all the gifts loaded up and taken to another location." Gavin turned to the front door, unaware of her distress. "I don't like having unchecked boxes here."

"Sir." A young man in a dark suit, sweat beading his forehead, lifted a hand to signal Gavin from the foyer. "We need your assistance."

Gavin strode toward him. "What is it, John?"

"Odd package, sir." John gestured toward the front room. "Needs to be checked out."

Gavin diverted swiftly to the front room. Mia followed and stopped right behind him in the doorway. Several dozen gifts sat piled on a large wood table. Most of them were elaborately wrapped in expensive paper and tied with silver and gold ribbons. Others were less fancy, packaged in various patterns of *Congratulations!* paper.

An odd smell permeated the room, something overly sweet and sickly.

"That one, sir." John pointed to a lumpy package at the edge of the table.

Hand-wrapped with thick pieces of tape, the package bore a white card scrawled with Luke and Polly's names. A stain bled through the paper, making an oily mark.

Gavin cursed beneath his breath. "Don't touch it."

He stalked toward the reception hall, gesturing sharply at two of his men as he spoke into his mic. "Secure the area. I want everyone evacuated, but not a single person senses anything is wrong. Close all vents. No one goes into the front room. Execute protocol stat."

Mia ran after him. "What should I do?"

He threw her a glare so cold it iced her heart over. "Get out of here. *Now.*"

His voice was like the strike of a whip. Mia turned and fled, gripping her skirts as she descended the front steps. Behind the villa, the guests were gathering on the expansive lawn, still unaware of the impending fireworks show.

She'd tell the musicians to begin playing in the hopes of distracting the guests from sensing anything was amiss. At least she could be of some small help. Even if Gavin didn't want her help anymore.

She rounded the side of the villa, unable to convince herself that her sudden reality check about Gavin was just hurt feelings. Maybe she'd even known the harsh truth all along and needed to be stripped of her silly illusions.

Blinking back tears, she started toward the lawn. A shadow stepped in front of her. Alarmed, she skidded to a halt. Trees blocked the bright lights of the garden, throwing this side of the villa into shadows.

Mia took a step back. Her heart pounded. The figure moved forward and stepped into a thin stream of light.

Shock flooded her. "Danny?"

He smiled. Dressed in a tan suit and tie, his curly hair slick with gel, he didn't look nearly as polished as many of the other guests, but no one would think to question his presence as one of Polly's friends.

Except he wasn't...was he?

"What are you doing here?" She tried to remember if there had been any Dannys on the guest list.

"Just celebrating a joyful event." He spread his arms out, his smile widening. "After you shot down my offer to be your date, I hooked up with another one of your less picky friends. Turned out she didn't have a *plus one* to the wedding yet and was more than happy to bring me along."

Mia took a few more steps back, taking some solace in the knowledge that there were plenty of people around—unlike during the incident in the parking lot. Except none of the guests were likely to notice anything beyond the thick trees separating the garden from the sideyard.

Her heels sank into the soft grass. Voices rose from the garden as more guests descended the terrace steps, many of them carrying drinks and champagne glasses.

"So could I at least get a dance tonight?" Danny asked.

For every step back she took, he moved toward her. Adrenaline charged through her. She turned and dashed back to the front of the villa.

"Not this time, bitch."

She gasped and was yanked to a halt. Her feet went out from under her. Danny fisted the back of her gown, pulling her upright. He hauled her back against him, snaking his hand up the front of her body and seizing her throat.

"Gotcha," he said, a smile still in his voice. "Now let's find out just how far that fucker Stone is willing to go."

"What do you want with Luke?" Mia struggled against his grip.

"Bastard stole my idea for a candy product." Danny tightened his hand on her throat. "Zigzag Candy was *my* idea. Now he's getting rich off it and not giving me a penny."

"Luke didn't steal anything from you."

His grip tightened. She inhaled, trying not to panic at the restriction of her air flow. She kicked back with her heel. He darted away just before impact. Her lungs began to hurt. He dragged her backward into the shadow of the house, his breath rasping in her ear.

She couldn't breathe. Black spots swam before her eyes. She clutched his arm, digging her fingernails in. He was stronger than he looked, his sinewy muscles hard as rock.

"Wait," she gasped. "I know Luke...I can talk to him for you..."

"Too late. He doesn't want to answer my letters? Well, he'll pay now."

Before Mia could respond, an explosion ruptured the night.

ucking fireworks.

Gavin gritted his teeth. A spray of red and gold flared across the sky from the boat stationed several miles offshore. The guests gasped and *ohhed* with astonishment as the display began.

Much as he hated the noise and flare, Gavin took consolation in the fact that everyone, even the kitchen staff and assistants, were all a safe distance from the villa and entirely focused on the surprise of the fireworks.

"All rooms are clear, sir." John hurried to his side.

Gavin nodded, his attention on the computer displaying the path of the remote sensor they'd sent into the front room. Tension thickened the air. The laser flashed onscreen as the device approached the suspicious package.

"Detecting liquid materials, but no chemical agents, sir," one of the men said. "No electronics, radioactivity, or smoke either."

The robot picked up the package as the laser and x-ray scanned the interior. A green light flashed on the screen: all negative for hazardous material.

One of the men moved toward the door. Gavin held out a hand to stop him.

"Sir..."

Gavin's shoulders tightened. Fuck if he wasn't going down with his ship, if need be. He knelt beside the package, which the robot had put on the floor. The overly sweet smell hit his nose, the oily patch on the paper spreading. He unfastened the tape and tore it off the package.

The box contained a set of essential oils, incense, and candles. One of the bottles was broken, leaking through the box and paper. Gavin tossed it aside and stood, giving the others an *all clear* signal.

"Sweep the rest of the area," he ordered.

He left the villa and crossed to the garden, every one of his nerves still on high alert. They'd done a thorough sweep of the grounds earlier that day, but the fact that something had gotten past him—

Fireworks blazed in the sky, a riotous display of color and light. Music danced through the air along with the hum of conversation and laughter. Gavin took a breath, glad at least that the scare hadn't affected his friend's wedding.

He made his way through the crowd, keeping one eye out for Mia while he listened to his men verifying the *all clear* throughout the villa. Where was she? He was an ass for having snapped at her in the adrenaline-charged moment of discovering something had slipped his attention.

He'd known she was focused on her friend's happiness, that it wasn't her job to relay important communications. And yet he'd hated the implication that this wasn't *their* project, the one they'd made happen together, with her eye for beauty and his security expertise. A manifestation of their two worlds.

If they could create it through a wedding, then maybe—

He returned to the villa and paused on the terrace, which gave him an overview of the mingling guests. He could have picked Mia out of a stadium crowd. The fact that he couldn't find her among the wedding guests made him increasingly uneasy.

She had to be outside. He'd ordered her to get out of the villa, and he didn't care how harsh his order had been. All he cared about was her safety.

He started down the steps. A flash of blue caught the corner of his eye behind a line of trees. He turned, instinctively rounding the side of the house to an area blocked off from the gardens. He froze.

"Get Stone over here." The young man holding Mia moved into a stream of light. His hand was gripping her throat, the other wrapped around her waist.

Gavin held up his hands in a nonthreatening gesture. Mia was holding the kid's arm, her expression scared, but not panicking. By contrast, the boy was highly agitated, his pupils dilated and sweat dripping down his temple.

"What's your name?" Gavin asked.

"Danny." His gaze darted past Gavin to the crowd. "Where the fuck is Stone?"

"Let her go first, and I'll get Mr. Stone."

"No way."

Gavin's pulse raced. Danny's knuckles were whitening on Mia's throat. Her breathing rasped through the air. The noise of the crowd receded into the distance. He stepped forward. Danny moved, and a knife blade flashed.

Shit. Gavin stopped. Sweat trickled down his neck.

"Don't fucking try it." Danny dragged Mia backward, moving his hand from her throat to put the knife blade at her jugular. "He screwed me over, and now you're all going to pay."

"You didn't plant a bomb here, Danny. We both know that."

"You don't know shit," the boy snapped. "That fucker Stone owes me millions. Millions. He stole from me. And if he won't pay me what I'm owed, I'll kill his whole goddamned family."

Mia gasped. The pressure of the knife increased, drawing a thin red line at her throat. Gavin smothered his rising fear.

"All right, Danny," he agreed. "But you know I can't leave you alone with her. Let her go, and I'll get Mr. Stone for you. I was just talking to him. I know exactly where he is."

"Exterior circle is clear, sir," one of his men said into the earpiece.

"Danny, I need my radio. It's in my belt. I'm going to reach down and get it, all right?"

"And tell everyone what's going on?" Danny shook his head, pulling Mia backward. "You reach for your radio, I slash her throat."

Gavin held up his hands again. He didn't—couldn't—look at Mia. If he saw how scared she was, he'd lose his mind.

"Danny, I can't go anywhere until I know she's safe," he said. "At least take the knife away from her throat."

"Don't tell me what to do!" Danny yelled.

The knife dug in harder. Mia flinched, her skin draining of color. Adrenaline charged through Gavin's body. He was a split-second from rushing forward and tackling Danny when Mia spoke.

"I'm sorry, Danny." Despite her fear, her voice was steady and gentle.

The unexpected remark made Danny hesitate. "What the hell are you sorry for?"

Mia loosened her grip on his arm and stroked her hand across it, her gaze briefly meeting Gavin's. He knew in an instant what she was doing. Pride flickered beneath his fear.

"I'm sorry for all this shit you've been through." Mia moved her fingers to touch Danny's bare wrist. "I'm sorry we didn't get to know each other better sooner. We have a lot in common. We like to have fun, go out, meet new people. And when I told you I was seeing someone, I didn't tell you it was just a casual fling with a guy who's the polar opposite of me. A man I don't have anything in common with."

Her gaze shifted to Gavin again. He felt like a shard of ice had just penetrated his chest.

"So why did you turn me down?" Danny asked, his grip on her as tight as ever.

"Maybe it was a mistake," Mia said. "But you and me, Danny, we get each other, you know?" She covered his hand—the one holding the knife at her throat—with her own. "We're both looking for jobs, starting a career, trying out different things. I'm not surprised you came up with a great idea for a candy product but didn't get any credit for it. You've always been a really smart guy."

"Right?" He shook his head, his eyes darkening with new anger. "What the fuck is it with people always keeping me down? I didn't get that sales job either. Fucking *entry level*. I don't get something soon, I'll be slinging burgers for the rest of my life."

"It totally sucks," Mia said sympathetically. "You try so hard and no one gives you a break. Except for this one."

In a move so fast it happened in a blur, she drew her knee forward and slammed her foot back, her sharp, pointed heel making contact with Danny's kneecap. He yelped in both surprise and pain, his hold on her loosening.

Gavin lunged forward. Mia yanked herself free of Danny's grip and stumbled back. Danny lashed out with the knife, slashing Gavin across the arm. The blade tore his sleeve, but didn't penetrate far. Gavin grabbed Mia and shoved her behind him.

Danny turned, his eyes wild with rage. He charged toward Gavin, knife first. Gavin stepped aside, grabbed the younger man into a headlock, and gripped his wrist. The knife fell to the ground.

"You're done." Gavin took a pair of cuffs from his belt and latched them around Danny's wrists.

"You sonuvabitch," Danny spat, struggling to escape his grip. "You can't do this. I'll fucking kill you all."

"Yeah, I've heard that before," Gavin muttered.

Still holding Danny, he turned to ensure Mia was still behind him. Pale and shaken, her hair a mess, she stood shaking in a delayed reaction. He ran an assessing gaze over her, forcing himself to remain clinically detached. Aside from the cut on her throat, she appeared physically unhurt.

Relief flooded his chest, hard and fast. He hauled Danny around to the front to the villa, ignoring his screech of pain, and gestured to one of his men.

"Get him to the police department," he ordered. "I'll call in to the chief letting him know what happened and that you're on the way."

"You asshole!" Limping, Danny wrestled futilely with the brawny security officer who led him to the truck. "You'll never get away with this, and neither will Luke Stone."

Gavin made a quick call to the chief of police, then checked in with his second-in-command to explain the situation. He returned to Mia. She stood with her arms wrapped around herself.

The sight of her—vulnerable, strong, and more precious to him than breathing—hit him deep in a place he hadn't known existed. He stopped in front of her, his hands fisting, suppressing the urge to haul her into his arms, hold her tight, touch every part of her to ensure she was okay.

He no longer had that right. He'd vowed that everyone would stay safe on his watch. And yet the *one person* who had gotten hurt was the woman who now meant more to him than his own life. He hated himself for not protecting her.

"Are you...are you all right?" he asked.

She gave a short nod, pressing her lips together. "I assume we're not going to blow up?"

"Everything is fine. The package was a present that had gotten broken. Scented oils and incense."

She gave a faint, humorless smile. "I suppose that could be dangerous, in the right circumstances."

Gavin's insides iced over. He couldn't stand seeing her like this—remote and closed-off. She was in shock, but it was more than that, like she wanted to keep him away. He should have been almost grateful for the fact that she'd already figured out she needed to keep him at a distance, but all he felt was pain. Words tangled in his throat.

"I'm sorry I ignored you for so long," he finally said. "You didn't deserve my coldness, not a warm, lovely girl like you. You're...you're like sunshine."

She looked past his shoulder, her eyes growing suspiciously bright. "If only you knew how many times during the past year I wished you'd say something like that to me. Or even just *Hello, Mia.* Anything."

He started to speak, but she shook her head. A tear ran down her cheek. His body reacted like he was going into battle—everything tightening, locking down. He struggled to breathe.

"I know you t-thought I was this flakey little airhead," she said, her breath hitching, "but every time I saw you sitting at the bakery, so stoic and rigid with nothing but your laptop and a stupid cup of black coffee, I just felt like you *needed* me."

Gavin's heart almost broke in half. For a second, he didn't even know what the feeling was. He'd never felt the machinations of his heart as much in his whole life as he had in two weeks with Mia Donovan.

He started toward her. She held up a hand. He stopped.

"Yes, I wanted to get a reaction out of you by flirting," she continued, wiping her cheek with the back of her hand. "But I also felt like you needed...*light*. You needed to loosen up, have fun, put some sugar in your coffee, for god's sake. And maybe I was foolish to think I was the one who could help you do all that, but I just liked you so much. I liked your strength, how you're so dedicated to Luke and Sugar Rush, how successful you are at your job. I liked that you focus so intently on everything you do, how you command such respect from your team. I liked that you give people your undivided attention when they're talking to you.

"But I didn't realize until we got together that everything I felt was more than admiration. More than wanting to make you my project and loosen you up. I've been falling in love with you for over a year. And the moment you finally kissed me is when I fell in love with my whole heart."

He couldn't speak. For a brief, glorious instant, he rejoiced in her confession, ached to return it, to admit that the intensity of all his feelings for her could be distilled into the single word *love*.

Then that instant was eclipsed by the hard, crushing reality of *them*. Mia Donovan with her genuine goodness, her natural facility with people, and her longing to create beauty didn't need a man who would crush her vision with his instinctive, unyielding need to eradicate potential threats. A man who saw danger in helium balloons, pizza delivery, and scented oils. A man who had failed to protect her.

"Mia." Her name was his breath, the beat of his heart, every single part of him that saw a reason for light and hope. "I can't…"

"You can," she said. "But you won't."

No, he wouldn't. Couldn't.

"I love you, Gavin." She gazed at him, her eyes filled with an unbearable sorrow that speared him to the core. "But I see now that you'll never let yourself admit that you just might love me, too." She turned to the steps of the terrace, her shoulders rigid. "You should get back to your security team. They need you."

"I need *you*."

But by the time Gavin got the words out, choked and twisted, Mia was gone.

CHAPTER 18

*I*t took her half an hour to stop shaking and to suppress the tears. Mia closed herself up in the upstairs bridesmaids' room, knowing Gavin wouldn't come after her while he was still on duty. Even if he wanted to. She gulped down a few breaths and gathered the remnants of her composure.

Though she hated that her memory of Polly's wedding would be stained with both Danny's assault and a break-up with Gavin, Mia took some consolation in the knowledge that she—and Gavin—had been the only ones affected.

As far as she knew, thanks to the unobtrusiveness of Knight Security, no one else was even aware that there had been an "incident." Gavin would have to give an explanation to the Stones and Danny's date, but Mia knew he'd come up with something plausible. The rest of the wedding party and guests had had a lovely evening and would only rave about the eldest Stone brother's nuptials.

And sooner or later, Mia would have had to face the reality of her and Gavin's relationship. Maybe it was better that it happened here, in the midst of a pure celebration of love, where she could see the futility of *Mia & Gavin* with painfully sharp clarity.

After taking a few moments to fix her hair and makeup, she retrieved her chiffon scarf from the reception hall to conceal the thin knife line at the base of her throat. Then she forced a smile on her face and returned to the garden, where the party was winding down after the fireworks show.

"There you are." Polly came toward her, as radiant as she'd been at the beginning of the day. "That was incredible. I can't believe you and Hannah kept it a secret from us."

She linked her arm through Mia's and started back inside to the reception hall. The security team patrolled both the perimeter of the gardens and the foyer, but she knew Gavin wouldn't have allowed the guests back inside unless he'd personally declared the entire place safe.

The guests bustled around, still exclaiming over the fireworks as they finished up leftover cake. Gavin was nowhere to be seen, though several of his men hovered around the room, like shadows in their black suits.

As the party wound down, Mia went upstairs to fetch Polly's overnight travel bag. The newlyweds were heading to San Francisco to stay at the Four Seasons hotel for the night before leaving for their honeymoon the following morning. They made the rounds, saying goodbye and thanking all their friends, before Luke's brother Tyler ushered everyone onto the villa steps for the couples' final departure.

A shiny, classic Mustang, personally restored by Tyler as a wedding present to the happy couple, waited at the base of the steps. Hand-in-hand, Luke and Polly made their way out amidst cheers and a rainshower of dried flower petals.

Mia applauded and cheered along with everyone else, resolutely setting aside her own dismay in favor of happiness for her friend and genuine delight that the whole event had been such a success. Most of other guests began leaving, collecting wraps and wedding favors from the reception hall before making their way to the parking lot.

The bridesmaids, groomsmen, and other family members lingered in the hall, finishing their drinks and talking. The band was still playing, the musicians having been treated to plenty of food and drinks as well. Hannah and Evan were on the dance floor, their arms wrapped around each other as they moved to the strains of *Make You Feel My Love*. Everyone looked happy, tired, and utterly content.

Mia sank into a chair, fatigue washing over her. Soon the trauma of the night's events would hit her, but for now she tried to hold on to the feeling of pleasure that everything had gone well for Polly, Luke, and the other guests.

"Mia."

She looked up. Julia Bennett walked toward her, magnificently elegant in a beaded Oscar de la Renta dress that made her look like a classic movie star. An older woman with steel-gray hair, also exquisitely dressed and coiffed, was at her side.

Mia got to her feet instinctively, like she was in the presence of royalty. "Hello, Julia. I hope everything went well from your perspective?"

"That's why I want to talk to you, actually." Julia waved for Mia to sit back down, as she and the other woman pulled out chairs at the table. "This is my dear friend Priscilla. She and her husband own the Hundred Acre Vineyards down in Temecula, and they're celebrating their fortieth anniversary this October."

"That's wonderful. Congratulations."

"We'd like to have the party at the vineyard," Priscilla explained, scrolling through her phone. "Perhaps two hundred people or so. Wine tasting, of course, and a dinner. We'll have a professional photographer, and *Wine* magazine will be on hand to write an article about it."

"Sounds lovely." Though she was a little confused by the conversation, Mia accepted the phone Priscilla extended to her.

Onscreen were several photos of a sprawling, gorgeous vineyard and Italian-style stone villa.

"I haven't decided on the entertainment yet, but music and dancing is always well-received," Priscilla continued.

Mia agreed, handing the phone back as she glanced at Julia. To her surprise, Julia was watching her with faint amusement, as if she knew a secret Mia didn't.

"Priscilla is interested in hiring you to plan the anniversary party for her," Julia finally explained.

Mia blinked. "Seriously?"

"Seriously," Julia replied, the derisive undercurrent of her voice warning Mia not to sound like a teenager. "We've all been quite impressed with how well you planned the wedding. Every-thing was flawless, from the decorations to the ceremony itself and the timeline. I've heard nothing but compliments all evening, and I'm personally grateful to you for having done justice to my eldest nephew's wedding. I'm sure you know I was wary when Polly refused to let me hire a wedding planner, but she made a hundred percent right decision. You did a beautiful job, Mia. Thank you."

If Mia hadn't been so stunned by the words, she would have started to cry all over again. Instead she just sat there, staring at Julia in disbelief. Just the *thank you* from Julia Bennett would have been more than she'd hoped for, but that combined with all the rest of it...

She bit her lip, which had started to tremble.

"I was happy to do it," she managed to say. "I'm just glad it all turned out so well."

"Priscilla asked me earlier this evening who'd done the event," Julia continued. "And when I heard she was planning the anniversary party, I suggested that she talk to you about it. She knows that you're starting out, but I assured her you were equal to the task. And of course, this wedding is an excellent referral in and of itself."

"It most certainly is," Priscilla agreed, opening her Chanel handbag. "And I value Julia's advice and opinion implicitly. Here's my card. Give me a call next week, and we can get started."

"I will." Mia took the business card with a shaking hand. "I'd be honored to help with your anniversary party. Thank you so much for trusting me."

"You clearly have a talent for creating beautiful events." Priscilla stood, looping her handbag around her arm. "We'll speak soon."

She headed off toward a rotund, portly man who was lingering by the bar. Julia stood as well, eyeing Mia pointedly.

"I don't make such recommendations lightly," she said. "Don't screw this up."

"I promise I won't."

Julia gave a short nod before turning on her heel and striding away like a queen exiting court. Though Mia would never have the other woman's sharp bite and haughtiness, she couldn't help feeling that she kind of wanted to be like Julia Bennett when she grew up. Just a little.

Excitement broke through her shock and her earlier dismay. She glanced around the room, wishing she could tell someone about the jumpstarting of her business, but everyone was paired up, and she was reluctant to intrude.

Instead she walked back upstairs to retrieve her things from the bridesmaids' room, grateful that the night had ended on a positive note. She changed into yoga pants and a T-shirt, packed up her dress and all the hair and makeup supplies she'd brought, and headed down to the parking lot.

As she loaded up her trunk, she caught sight of Gavin standing on the front steps, deep in conversation with his second-in-command. Garden lights illuminated his broad shoulders and glinted off his dark hair.

Longing seized her, the desperate instinct to run to him as fast as she could, leap into his arms, and share the good news with him. The opportunity that might never have happened if he hadn't pushed her to recognize her strengths.

She wanted him to laugh and say he'd known all along that she was capable of such great things. She wanted him to hug her tightly and tell her how proud he was of her.

He turned in her direction, but from the distance Mia couldn't tell if he saw her in the darkened lot. She did, however, feel the arc of heat and desire that crackled between them every time their eyes met.

She tore her gaze from him and got into her car, forcing herself not to look back as she drove away.

ou'll never let yourself admit that you just might love me, too.

Her words, her musical voice, ran incessantly through him. He didn't know what to do with that statement, where to fit it in the narrow corridors and angles of his mind and heart. But it was no surprise that Mia Donovan was the only person who had ever seen past his corroded layers to the truth at the very center of him.

Gavin still didn't dare to believe it was *love*. He'd never been in love before. Could it happen this way—in slow, steady increments over the course of a year, like drops of water filling a bucket?

Had he started to fall in love with Mia the instant he first saw her sitting on the bakery counter, swinging her leg and eyeing him with interest? Then when their gazes met, and he first heard her voice?

And with every moment after—when she brought him his coffee-with-no-sugar order and lingered by his chair, and he inhaled the scent that belonged only to her. When he overheard her cheerful chatter about new clubs and happy hours. When she showed up at Wild Child on a moment's notice to help out when an employee called in sick. When she twirled a lock of daffodil-sunshine hair around her finger and made a throaty, suggestive remark that went straight to his blood.

When a homeless man wandered into the bakery, and she fixed him a sandwich before giving him cash from her purse. When she firmly told Polly she wanted to take over the wedding plans because she saw that Polly was running herself ragged doing too much. When she wore new flowered tights or a sweater that hugged her perfect breasts. When she watered the bakery plants and took special care to turn them toward the light.

Every single one of those moments, and countless more, had slowly, steadily, filled Gavin's heart to the point that his entire day had been colored with anticipation over when he'd see Mia again. He hadn't dared to think he'd ever cross the invisible line he'd drawn between them, until the wedding had forced him to.

Or given him a great excuse.

And when he finally spoke to Mia, kissed her, touched her, cooked her dinner...she became part of his world. His *whole* world. The best, most all-encompassing part of him.

If that wasn't love...then what the hell *was*?

The questions and thoughts buzzed relentlessly through his mind, even when he was working. That alone was a measure of how desperate he was for Mia. The wedding was over, but Knight Security still had contracts to fulfill so there was no shortage of tasks. And yet through it all, he couldn't get her out of his head.

He'd never be able to get her out of his heart.

Two weeks after Luke and Polly's wedding, he was running himself into the ground with twenty-hour workdays. Walking back into his neutral, silent house was like entering a mausoleum.

He shed his coat and went to pour himself a scotch, but the liquor tasted bitter and sour. He tossed it into the sink and opened the freezer, digging out a carton of strawberry ice cream that he'd bought with Mia in mind.

He scooped a pile of ice cream into a bowl and sank down in front of the TV, flicking the channels before stopping on a romantic comedy that, of course, reminded him of the girl who'd stolen his heart.

Christ. He stared at the screen, everything in him flattened and cold. Without Mia, the *bad stuff* had returned full-force, the blistering nightmares waking him from shallow sleep. He'd taken to coloring to ease his mind, having bought all of Mia's granny's coloring books. Filling in the illustrations of fairytale lands and secret gardens had become a balm over the scorching burn of his past.

But nothing eased his regret over Mia. The pain of losing her.

Thoughts of her were an exquisite torture. Gavin jacked off to a thousand fantasies that were even more potent than before since he now had firsthand knowledge of her gorgeous body. He knew the incredible sensation of sinking his cock into her, of her tightening around him, taking him deep. He knew her hot breath on his skin, her hair wrapped around his fist, the sight of her body bouncing with every thrust.

He came fast and hard every time he let himself fantasize about her, but he was left with a hollowness darker than any he'd known. Because she'd shown him what was *possible*. What he couldn't have.

He went to work at six the next day, not caring that he spent the morning growling and snapping at his men, who never gave less than their best. He finally holed himself up in his office at noon, hating that he was acting like a bear with a wounded paw and yet not knowing how to get out of it.

"Hey, man."

Gavin looked up from his desk as Luke walked in, all loose-limbed and tan from two weeks on the Majorca coast with his new wife.

"Hey." He stood to shake Luke's hand. "Welcome back. Guess I don't need to ask if you had a good time."

Luke grinned and dropped into a chair. "Only bad part was having to come back."

Gavin sat back down and removed his glasses, resisting the urge to rub his sandpapery eyes. "Back to work yet?"

"Not until Monday." Luke eyed him speculatively. "You look like hell."

No wonder, considering he was living in it again. He stacked some folders on his desk, for the sake of something to do.

"That kid Danny took a deal. He'll undergo a psych eval, do some time." He squinted at his computer screen. "The judge issued a restraining order, so I'm guessing he'll get out of town once he's released. Won't be for a long time, though."

Luke nodded.

Gavin didn't like the way his friend was still looking at him, like he knew something Gavin didn't.

Maybe he did. Apprehension seized Gavin's chest. Mia was Polly's best friend. What if Luke had heard that Mia was dating some dickwad kid or had—

He blocked that thought and stood, grabbing his suit jacket. "I gotta go. You need something else?"

"Just wanted to debrief the wedding security, see if there's anything else we need over at the Sugar Rush campus."

"I'll send you a report. I need to go. I'm meeting your aunt over at the villa to review security for her Cream of the Crop bachelor auction."

"Ah, the annual event." Luke grinned. "Has she tried to recruit you again?"

"I'm handling security." Gavin snapped his briefcase shut. "And I don't do auctions, especially not bachelor auctions. Let me know if you have any questions about the report."

He left the office, not caring if he was being rude. Julia Bennett's annual auction of the "most eligible bachelors in the

Bay Area" always attracted a large, high-class crowd that was treated to cocktails, dinner, and many cream-filled desserts after they bid for dates with the men. All proceeds went to the charitable Rebecca Stone Foundation.

Knight Security had provided security for the annual event in the three years since it had started, but despite the fact that Gavin was on duty, Julia always tried to cajole him into participating as one of the bachelors. She also always failed.

He parked in the lot of the Spanish-style villa, blocking memories of Mia in her maid of honor gown, lighting up the room with her smile, then the dark, scared look on her face when that little fucker Danny held a knife to her throat...

Gavin's fists clenched as he made his way up the steps of the villa. Julia was in the courtyard, a tablet nestled in her arm. She glanced up at his approach, and they exchanged greetings.

"We're offering fifty extra tickets this year, so we need to reassess the seating arrangements and catwalk," Julia explained. "We'll also have extra tables inside and likely more staff on hand for the dessert table. And I'm closing a deal to have Rick Patterson from the Giants participate as the star celebrity bachelor."

"I'll have to coordinate with his security team," Gavin said. "And I need to see the full set of plans."

"I'll send you his security guy's contact info. Mia has all the plans."

His insides twisted. "Uh...Mia?"

"Mia Donovan." Julia typed something on her tablet, then pulled a business card from her leather bag. "She's helping plan the event this year."

Gavin studied the crisp white business card with an elegant dark purple font announcing: *Mia Donovan, Event Planner*. Pride swelled in his chest.

"I connected her with the woman who owns the Hundred Acre Vineyards, and Mia is planning a blow-out anniversary party," Julia continued. "She's getting dozens of calls from people who attended the wedding, asking about her services and prices."

"That's great." Gavin slipped the card into his breast pocket, right next to his heart. "She'll do a good job."

"You can talk to her about the seating arrangements and agenda." Julia put her tablet into her bag and glanced at her watch. "Polly told me you and Mia worked together on the wedding security issues, and since everything went off without a hitch, I have complete confidence that you'll do the same with the auction."

Christ. He couldn't work with Mia again. He didn't have the willpower, not where she was concerned. He was crawling across a scorching desert, parched and blistering with heat. She was an oasis—cool, clear water; lush green plants; sweet, tempting fruit. He'd never be able to resist her.

He'd send one of his men to talk to her, get the info. Then Gavin could review it in the isolation of his office like the fucking coward he was.

"I'll set up a meeting with her," he said.

"You can talk to her right now." Julia nodded toward the villa.

Gavin's heart crashed against his ribs. He turned slowly. Mia descended the steps to the courtyard, a vision of beauty in a pale blue suit and heels, her long hair flowing around her shoulders like silk.

The sight of her almost brought him to his knees. Somehow, using whatever self-control he had left, he managed to keep his expression impassive.

She looked up from the notepad she was carrying, her gaze meeting his with a force that felt like a lightning strike. Surprise widened her eyes for an instant before a mask settled over her lovely features. She tore her gaze from Gavin and turned to the young man walking beside her, who Gavin just realized was even there.

His muscles tensed. The kid looked familiar, and Gavin

remembered he'd been to Wild Child a few times. As they neared, Mia's voice drifted to him like music.

"...we'd prefer to do the run-through a few days in advance of the event, so we have time to make necessary changes," she said to the guy, who was nodding and scribbling notes.

Then she stopped beside Julia and regarded him coolly.

"Mr. Knight." Mia extended her lavender-tipped hand. "A pleasure to see you again."

"You as well, Miss Donovan." He closed his hand around hers, gratified to see heat flare to her cheeks at the contact, her eyes darkening a shade. At least he wasn't the only one still affected by what they'd once had. Except that she looked a hell of a lot better than he felt, and the guy beside her was standing way too fucking close to her, even leaning to look at her as he spoke.

Gavin tightened his grip on his briefcase handle. He tried to focus on what Julia was saying.

"Nathan is facilitating the open bar." Julia gestured to the kid. "He's a friend of Mia's. And she has all the details so far about the seating and parking. I'm sure you'll find it's not much different from the wedding. Just keep me in the loop as you move forward."

She nodded her goodbyes and returned to the villa, lifting the phone to her ear.

"We're planning to set the bar up there." Nathan indicated the fountain. "Julia had wanted it closer to the foyer, but Mia said there might be safety issues if it creates a bottleneck at the entrance."

"Mia is right." Gavin couldn't stop himself from looking at her. Drinking her in.

Her color heightened under his scrutiny. She glanced at Nathan.

"I'll go over everything with Mr. Knight and get back to you," she said. "You should check out the kitchen, find out what you might be able to store there."

Nathan nodded and trotted off, clearly eager to do her bidding. Once the kid was gone, a thick silence fell. Gavin wanted to step closer to Mia, touch her, wind a lock of hair between his fingers. *Kiss her*. He almost ached with the urge.

Instead, he said, "Congratulations on your business. Julia gave me your card."

Her perfect mouth twisted. "I couldn't have done it without you."

"Yes, you could have. You *did*."

"Only because you believed I could." Her gaze skirted past him. "Because you made me believe it too."

He wanted no credit for anything that gave Mia exactly what she deserved—a happy, promising future doing what she loved. Helping people celebrate. Creating beauty.

"I'm glad you're doing well," he said. "I want nothing but the best for you."

Mia returned her gaze to him, her green eyes suddenly glinting with a hard light.

"Oh, stop it," she snapped. "*You* were the best for me, Gavin Knight. And you didn't want what I could give you. So don't you dare tell me you want *the best* for me, not when you were the one who took it away."

Pain cracked his chest. Words snarled in his head. Finally all he could manage was, "I'm sorry."

"Sorry for what? Throwing away something that was *so good* for both of us?"

"Yes. And I'm sorry I failed you."

Mia blinked. She stepped back, a crease of confusion appearing between her eyebrows. "What are you talking about?"

"The wedding." Gavin's jaw clenched. "I didn't protect you. Every time I think about what could have happened to you, it's a goddamned nightmare. Of all the people at the wedding, *you* were the one I failed."

She stared at him, her lips parting. "I never...Gavin, you didn't *fail* me. You never have."

He tore his gaze from her, unable to stand looking into those green eyes that he wanted to lose himself in forever. His shoulders tight, he dragged a hand through his hair.

"Yes, I did. I'd vowed to protect you, and I didn't."

She shook her head, her expression shadowed with dismay. She stepped forward, closing the distance between them, resting her hand on the side of his face. Her touch undid him, warming all the cold corners of his soul, shocking him with the intensity of what he'd had and lost.

"Gavin Knight, you did not fail me." Mia brushed her thumb over his jaw, her eyes filled with sadness. "You *saved* me. In more ways than I can count. Since the day you finally spoke to me, we've been working together. On the wedding plans, on making each other happy, on feeling good, on lots of stuff. Even with Danny, you knew instinctively what I was doing, and you moved in at the exact right time. That's not failure. If you can look past your guilt, you might be able to admit that you and I made a pretty good team."

"We did."

She lowered her hand from his face and stepped away from him, spreading her arms out. "So?"

His mind blurred, broke into fragments. Like his nightmares, he caught glimpses of scenes, both real and unreal, except these were all so fucking perfect they stole his breath.

Mia coming to live with him. Making dinner for her every night. Turning his spare bedroom into an office for her, letting her decorate his austere house with pink sofa pillows and flowers. Falling asleep with her at his side, her hair spread over his chest. Always remembering to buy her favorite ice cream at the grocery store.

Flipping the coin of his life from the past to the future. With her.

"Hey, Mia!"

Gavin yanked himself from the fantasies. Nathan stood on the terrace, pointing to his watch.

"We gotta get moving," he called. "Peter just called from Asante, and they got a table for us but they can't hold the seats long. Happy hour starts in a few minutes. Whole gang is there."

Mia indicated she'd be just a minute before turning back to Gavin. Sorrow still darkened her expression. He let out the breath he hadn't know he'd been holding. *Asante.* If he'd found Danny before the wedding, none of it would have happened.

"I need to go," Mia finally said.

He nodded, remembering all that she was before *him*. Cheerful, flirty, happy. Safe.

Mia took a slow step back, her gaze containing a plea that he was too much of a coward to want to read. Instead, he just stood there while the only woman he'd ever loved turned and walked away from him a second time.

He wouldn't get another chance.

CHAPTER 20

So much for thinking that she'd never see Gavin again. She hadn't considered the reality that they were part of the same circle, now more than ever with her event planning business well off the ground. They were bound to run into each other under professional circumstances now and then.

They might even have to work together again—although she'd received an email from one of his other security operatives about the bachelor auction plans. Maybe Gavin was planning to dump her off on someone else if actual collaboration was required.

Coward.

Annoyed with herself at the uncharitable thought—because Gavin Knight was anything but a coward, even if he couldn't face the reality of his own damned heart—Mia took a sip of hot cocoa and forced her attention to her laptop screen.

In the three weeks since the wedding, she'd rearranged her apartment and turned half of her living room into a small but organized office complete with a sky-blue scalloped desk and wooden filing cabinet, a bookshelf filled with binders of event details, a wall calendar, and a bulletin board pinned with notes and photos.

With a few stumbles, she had developed an efficient organizational system to plan both the anniversary party and the Cream of the Crop auction, as well as a Christmas wedding and a child's tenth birthday party. Though she still battled nerves at the idea that people were actually paying her to plan and execute their celebration of once-in-a-lifetime moments, Mia was beyond grateful for both their trust and for everything that had led her onto this path.

Especially Gavin. Even before seeing him yesterday, not an hour had passed when she hadn't thought of him and his pained, "*I need you*" that still echoed inside her. She didn't want him to hurt—not anymore—but she didn't want herself to hurt either. And given their totally different approaches to life and apparent lack of ability to collaborate long-term, *hurt* was unavoidable unless they parted ways romantically.

Although *parting ways* had proven to be more than just hurtful. It was a pain gnawing at her from the center of her heart. She was able to keep it at bay while she worked, not wanting to give her new clients anything less than her hundred-percent focus and attention, but alone at night her longing for Gavin bloomed sharp and jagged.

Nothing, not even ice cream for dinner and all-night *Princess Bride* marathons had mitigated the simple, unbearably complex fact that she still loved him deeply. Maybe she always would. If Granny were alive, she'd tell Mia that falling in love was the most powerful way of *creating beauty* that she could dream of. Because what was more beautiful than love?

Being loved in return.

Which Gavin, the big stupid lug, did not remotely understand.

With a groan, Mia rose from her desk and opened the curtains. A bright blue sky skimmed over the rooftops, and a gleaming golden sun rose over the horizon. Just another perfect fall day in coastal California that brought her own cloudy mood into even sharper focus.

At least she had a meeting this afternoon with a florist to go over ideas for the anniversary centerpieces—flowers always made life brighter. Until the petals fell off, and they wilted and died.

Good lord. Too much more of this, and she'd have to go Goth with dyed black hair, tragic black clothes, and heavy eyeliner. That would never do.

She poured herself a bowl of cold cereal and ate it in front of her laptop as she reviewed her tasks for the day. Her phone buzzed with a text from Polly.

Can you stop by Rainsville Wild Child around 9—Ramona is making a delivery and I'm in Indigo Bay, just need help with the counter for about an hour.

Since Mia's first meeting wasn't until one, she texted back: *Sure. I'll head over soon.*

Polly's reply came right away:

Thanks! Also, can we have dinner Fri night, just you and me? Lotus Indian Cuisine? With all the wedding hoopla, we haven't gotten together much the past few months. I miss you.

Relief and pleasure filled Mia's chest. There was nothing she needed more right now than to commiserate with her best friend over fragrant curry and a bottle of wine.

I'd love that, she texted back.

Happy to have something to look forward to, she slipped her phone into her bag. She figured she could work the rest of the morning on her laptop at Wild Child after helping at the counter, then head to her meeting.

She dressed professionally in a pink pleated, tea-length skirt and tailored white blouse with a Peter Pan collar. She fastened her hair into a high ponytail and packed her laptop and necessary folders into her leather messenger bag.

She drove to the Rainsville branch of Wild Child, housed in a newly refurbished building with brightly colored awnings and flowerboxes. There was always a morning rush for Declairs when the doors first opened at six, but by now the crowd had settled into customers who lingered at the round tables with their coffee and pastries—talking, working, and reading.

"Lifesaver!" Ramona bowed in front of Mia, her tattooed arms outstretched and her ponytailed dreadlocks swinging. "I can't believe I forgot to put the delivery on the schedule. It's a three-tiered cake for the anniversary of the hardware store. You'll be okay alone?"

"Sure." Mia took a minute to admire the elaborate cake—meticulously decorated with fondant hammers, saws, wrenches, and screwdrivers.

As Ramona loaded the cake into the van, Mia pulled on a purple Wild Child apron and set about restocking the baskets in the glass display cases. She always enjoyed working at the bakery's front counter. Polly, who knew all about creating *warmth*, had turned Wild Child into a delightful, welcoming place with bohemian décor and local artwork, not to mention delicious pastries.

Mia bustled around refilling teacups, packaging cakes, filling éclairs with cream, and chatting with the regulars. She set a tray of vanilla cupcakes on the counter and loaded a pastry bag with strawberry buttercream. As she started to pipe the frosting onto the cakes, the wind chimes over the door jingled, signaling a customer.

Focused on finishing the perfect buttercream swirl, Mia didn't immediately look up. Then a deep male voice spoke, one that she still heard in her dreams.

"I'll have a caramel-chocolate mochaccino with extra chocolate, a shot of toffee syrup, vanilla whipped cream, and rainbow sprinkles," he said.

Mia straightened, her heart thumping so fast it was either about to take flight or burn out. Gavin stood on the other side of the counter, unbearably beautiful in a gray suit and tie, his dark hair gleaming and his gaze fixed on her.

"Plus a Declair," he added. "Please."

Her throat tightening, she couldn't get any words out. She didn't have any left. She'd said all she could possibly say to him— at least, until he gave her some words in return.

She went automatically to the coffee machine and started to steam the milk.

Wait...what?

"You want a caramel-chocolate mochaccino?" She turned to him in disbelief.

"With extra chocolate, toffee syrup, vanilla whipped cream, and rainbow sprinkles," he said. "The Mia Special."

"What happened to *black coffee, no sugar*?"

"Black coffee is getting dull," he said. "And I'm starting to like sugar."

A tiny hope nudged at Mia's heart. She tried to suppress it as she turned back to the coffee machine to make him her creation. She'd spent well over a year *hoping* for something to happen with Gavin. And when it finally had, she'd hoped even harder that it would last. Maybe, like words, she'd also used up all her hopes.

Except—who was she kidding? She was *made* of hope.

Even in her darkest hours after Granny died, Mia had clung to the belief that her grandmother was now painting the stars with bright colors and glitter. Even sitting in her claustrophobic cubicle at the insurance agency, she'd drawn smiley faces on the reports in the hopes that they'd brighten someone's day, especially in the face of an insurance claim.

She'd hoped for Polly's relationship with Luke to work. She'd hoped Wild Child would succeed. She'd hoped the best for her friends as they started new jobs and got married. She'd hoped her favorite Indian restaurant would start taking reservations, and that the dry cleaner would get the wine stain out of her blue floral skirt.

And for Gavin, she *still* hoped. Desperately. But that didn't mean she'd let down her guard, especially not the one she'd built around her heart.

She swirled whipped cream onto the mochaccino and decorated it with rainbow sprinkles before placing it on the counter in front of him. She fetched a Declair from the secret stash in the walk-in fridge, placed it on a plate, and set it next to the coffee.

"Five fifty," she said.

He handed her a twenty and waved away the change. He picked up the mochaccino and took a sip. To his credit, he didn't wince as the sweet-enough-to-hurt-your-teeth concoction hit his tongue. He merely set the mug down and nodded.

"Tasty," he remarked, with a slight cough.

Mia gestured to his mouth. His beautiful, well-shaped mouth that could produce such a gorgeous smile, and that she so loved to kiss and lick...

Down, girl.

"Whipped cream," she said.

Gavin reached for a napkin. Before he could bring it to his mouth, Mia wiped the cream off his upper lip with her fingers. Shivers raced clear up her arm. A hint of stubble abraded her fingertips, his breath touched her skin, and a thousand memories flooded her of all the delicious things he could do with that mouth.

Seriously. Down, girl.

His blue eyes flared with a light closely resembling the one that had flickered to life inside her the second she saw him standing there.

No. Heart guard.

She stepped back, shoving her hands into her apron pockets.

"What are you doing here, Gavin?"

"Hoping for a third chance."

She drew in a breath and looked at the strawberry-frosted cupcakes to conceal a surge of anticipation.

"Why?" she asked, managing to keep her voice steady.

He didn't respond. Ramona strode in from the kitchen, dusting off her hands and announcing the hardware store owner was thrilled with the cake.

"Thanks for helping out," she told Mia.

"No problem." Mia glanced at Gavin, knowing he wouldn't want to have a private conversation in such a public place. "Do you want to go somewhere else?"

"No," he said. "I can say what I need to say right here."

Ramona lifted an eyebrow, looking from Gavin to Mia and back again. She crossed her arms and leaned against the counter.

"Go for it," she invited.

Gavin bent to take something out of a paper bag resting at his feet. He set a ceramic pot on the counter in front of Mia. A few green shoots topped with brownish seed pods emerged from a layer of dirt.

"This is for you." He gestured to the pot as if he were presenting an elaborate floral bouquet.

Mia peered at the curved little shoots. "What are they?"

"Sunflowers," Gavin explained. "You can start them indoors and then plant them outside, so I figured it would be good for your apartment."

"Oh. Well, thank you."

"I wanted to get you something that would grow and bloom, so I didn't get cut flowers. And it's a flower that's like the sun, which reminds me of you."

Her hope flourished a little harder. The bakery had gone oddly quiet, as most of the customers had turned their attention to what was going on at the counter. Thankfully there was no one in line behind Gavin to interrupt him.

He reached into the bag again and produced a stack of her granny's coloring books, which he set beside the flowerpot. Mia picked one up and leafed through it. Every last one of the illustrations was meticulously colored, the images leaping from the page into bright, vibrant life.

Mia's throat tightened. Granny was smiling down on them from the rafters.

She set the book back on the pile, knowing the entire stack was colored in the exact same way.

"Is this how you've been spending your spare time?" she asked.

"When the rom-coms got a little too much for me," he admitted.

She smiled. Behind his glasses, his eyes warmed, though a hint of caution remained. He walked around the counter to approach her, closing his hands on her shoulders. His touch was like an anchor, a homecoming.

"I'm sorry," Gavin said, a shadow passing across his face. "I'm sorry for every single second I pretended to ignore you. Every instant I said or did something that hurt your feelings. I'm sorry I didn't realize sooner what an incredible gift you are. I'm sorry I didn't tell you every chance I had that you made my heart come back to life. That because of you, I can see a future that isn't only focused on work.

"I'm sorry I didn't realize sooner how you'd turn my life around, fill it with everything good. I'm sorry I didn't know I was the luckiest bastard on earth to have caught the attention of Mia Donovan, the girl who creates beauty in the world just by *existing*. I'm sorry I didn't do everything I could to hold on to you forever. I'm sorry I couldn't admit sooner that I love you, that you had my heart the minute you first looked at me."

Although Mia was well-versed in French romantic poetry, no sonnet or *rondeau* could compare to hearing those words from the man she still loved wildly. Light and air filled her whole body, lifting her heart like a balloon. In front of her, Gavin's face went all blurry behind her sudden sheen of tears.

"I know all that now." His throat worked with a swallow. "And I want to be with you, to give you everything you need. If you still want to be with me."

A heavy, expectant hush fell over the bakery. Mia didn't respond right away, not because she wanted to keep everyone waiting but because things with Gavin had *hurt*. Maybe she'd gotten a little huffy when he'd ignored her flirting, but that had been nothing like the pain at the realization that their differences would drive them apart. She didn't want to feel that kind of pain again.

He slid his hands down to hers. His hands were so big that hers were engulfed in his grip. Just one of the many things she loved about him—the fact that he could wrap himself fully around her.

"What changed your mind?" she asked.

"You did. You changed everything. My mind, my heart, my soul. You showed me what a future with you can look like, if I grab it. Turns out I like hot cocoa and the color pink. And that *Princess Bride* movie isn't bad."

"Hmm." She narrowed her eyes, even though her heart had most definitely taken flight and was now soaring over fields laden with sunflowers. "*Isn't bad* might not be enough for me. We'll have to work on that, maybe with a *Princess Bride* marathon and ice-cream sundaes."

"As you wish."

Well, that did it.

She closed the distance between them and slid her arms around his waist as applause burst around them. His eyes crinkling with a smile behind his glasses, Gavin slipped his hand under her chin and lowered his mouth to hers. Mia's whole being flared with anticipation, but the instant before their lips touched, a raucous noise broke through the air.

Her heart jolted, her arms tightening around Gavin. She jerked away from him to stare at the customers, all of whom had risen to their feet and were blowing noisemakers and horns, and firing off party poppers.

Rainbow confetti and streamers exploded throughout the bakery. The doors burst open, and Polly ran in, wielding a huge bouquet of multicolored helium balloons. Cheers, applause, and laughter rose like a tidal wave.

Her heart still hammering wildly, Mia's gaze flew to Gavin in both shock and concern about his reaction to the chaos. But he was only looking back at her and smiling, his blue eyes as warm as a summer sky.

"Surprise," he said.

"Gavin Knight." Mia laughed, pressing a hand to her chest. "I can't believe you arranged all this."

"Your mission to make me like surprises seems to have worked." He put his hand under her chin again and drew her closer. "But you're my best surprise of all."

This time, their lips met in a kiss that sizzled with love and countless promises. Mia curled her fingers into the back of his suit jacket, feeling his heart beating right against hers, their bodies fitting perfectly together.

Oh, beautiful destiny that always sets you on the right path to fulfilling your deepest wish.

Even working at Ye Olde Insurance Agency had had *a point* because without being stuck, she wouldn't have gotten unstuck. And she might never have found her way into Gavin Knight's arms, the place where she was meant to be.

"Miss Donovan." Gavin broke their kiss and slid his hand over her cheek, his eyes filled with all the things she'd longed to see— love, devotion, and a pure, warm tenderness reserved only for her. "I love you."

He bent to ease one arm beneath her legs and the other around her back. In a swift movement, he lifted her against him.

Mia gasped when her feet left the ground, though there was nowhere in the world she felt safer than cradled against Gavin's powerful chest.

"What are you doing?" She slipped her hand over his shoulder.

"Taking you home." He pulled her closer, his grip secure and possessive. "I'll come back for the sunflowers and balloons."

To continued applause and a rainshower of confetti, he strode to the open door with her in his arms. Mia couldn't stop smiling, exhilaration and love spinning through her like cotton candy.

"When did you become such a romantic?" she asked.

"When I started believing in epic, swashbuckling tales of true love," Gavin said. "That is to say, when I first met you."

He winked at her and stepped into the sunshine.

ABOUT THE AUTHOR

New York Times & USA Today bestselling author Nina Lane writes hot, sexy romances about professors, bad boys, candy makers, and protective alpha males who find themselves consumed with love for one woman alone. Originally from California, Nina holds a PhD in Art History and an MA in Library and Information Studies, which means she loves both research and organization. She also enjoys traveling and thinks St. Petersburg, Russia is a city everyone should visit at least once. Although Nina would go back to college for another degree because she's that much of a bookworm and a perpetual student, she now lives the happy life of a full-time writer.

www.ninalane.com

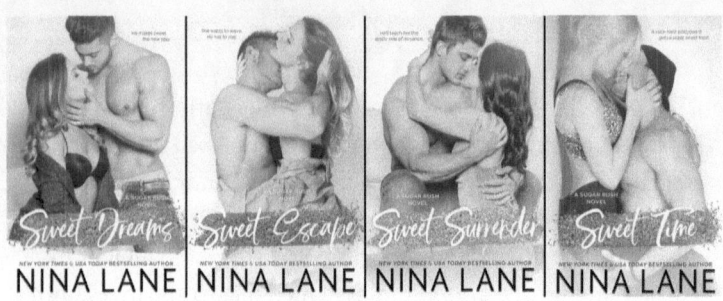

THE SUGAR RUSH SERIES
Sweet is the new sexy.

From the Stone family patriarch down to the youngest
bad boy, follow the lives and loves of the Sugar Rush men and the
women who bring them to their knees.

THE SPIRAL OF BLISS SERIES

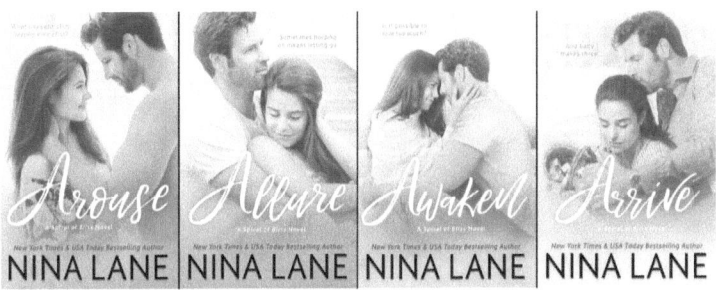

"Give me a kiss, beauty."

From an exhilarating crush to the intensities of marriage, Liv and Dean West embark on a passionate lifelong journey together. As the medieval history professor and his beloved wife face both personal challenges and painful battles, they never lose sight of the hope, humor, and devotion that belong only to them.

Liv and Dean's everlasting romance will melt your heart, turn you on, and enchant you with the power of a love to end all loves.

First we fell in love. Then we fell apart.

Shattered by tragedy a decade ago, two lovers fight the secrets that could destroy them.

"This book is a work of art."

A woman fleeing scandal. A town's mysterious recluse.

Lust and secrets collide in this provocative romance.